CORNUCOPIA

DEBRA DUNBAR

CHAPTER 1

I stood before a shimmering gateway amid the rubble that used to be an upscale mall in Columbia, Maryland. Irix was going to kill me for this. That is, if the elves or the demons on the other side of that gateway didn't kill me first.

"Are you going to go through or spend all of eternity staring at it?" The gate guardian asked me testily. He was an angel, but a minor type of angel that didn't really inspire any sort of awestruck respect. And he was a jerk. Although if I had to spend a hundred years in a pile of rubble staring at a gateway in case a demon came through, I'd probably be a jerk too.

"In a minute. I need to…prepare." There was nothing to prepare for. Walk through. Meet a demon escort on the other side. Go help a group of humans in Hel grow crops in what was fast becoming a desert. Try not to get killed. And in return for that, Irix would receive immunity.

Immunity was important, because Irix was one of those demons that angels such as this gate guardian were supposed to kill on sight. I loved Irix, and having him turned into a pile of sand by an angel would put a serious cramp in our relationship.

This whole no-demons thing meant we'd been sneaking around since we met. Every time things got dicey and one of us had to use our special abilities, angels came running. Which meant Irix had to high-tail it back to Hel. Which meant a separation of months that was making me cranky.

Of course, I wasn't technically supposed to be frolicking around on the human side of the gates either, but the angels liked elves, and in their eyes that's exactly what I seemed to be. It was to my advantage that my succubus half remained hidden to them. Although in Hel I'd be better off as a full succubus and not an exotic half-breed that would bring all kinds of unwanted attention and most likely my death.

Risk death and gain immunity for my beloved. It was a good bargain, in my opinion. I just needed to work up the nerve to walk through that gateway.

"Any day now, elf," the gate guardian drawled. He sat down on a chunk of concrete with rusty rebar sticking out of it and spread his wings. "Although I've no idea why you want to go back to Hel. You all just got here. And here is a whole lot better than Hel."

I'm sure it was. The elves had begun some strange migration from the land of the demons. I wasn't certain what spurred their exodus but the whole thing worried me. This was my safe space, where I could blend in the with humans, go to college, get a great job, make a future with my incubus boyfriend. Yes, I needed the energy generated through sexual activity to survive as a half-succubus, but as far as the humans were concerned, that just made me a bit on the slutty side. None of *them* was trying to kill me. But with a bunch of elves invading the place I'd always called home, that might change.

Maybe I should stay in Hel. Maybe I should stop procrastinating and walk through that gateway.

I took a deep breath, shut my eyes, and stepped forward. The first thing that hit me once the disorienting vertigo settled was the heat. It was a dry, dusty heat that settles into your pores and turns your hair into straw. There was a faint smell of dry grass mixed with an even fainter aroma of stagnant water. It might be dry where I stood, but not too far off was water. Yucky, slime-filled, bug-infested, water, but still water.

The dizzy, puke-on-the-ground feeling had passed so I opened my eyes and looked around. Hel was…. well, it was hell. don't know why I expected anything different. I'd read Dante, I'd heard the sermons, but nothing prepared me for the desolation and the stark contrast between the 'kingdoms' before me. I stood in a land of oppressive heat, red sand and packed clay burning my feet clear through the rubber soles of my sneakers. The air felt thick and heavy. It was like an electric blanket whose warmth seeped through my skin and into my veins. Something about the atmosphere here sparked a part of me – no doubt the succubus part.

In the distance I could see that the desert eventually became pockmarked with brownish plants. The scent of fetid, swampy water hit my nose with more strength than it originally had when I'd stepped through the gateway. It told me the place the demons called home wasn't all a dry, fiery pit. But that was in the distance. Where I stood there wasn't the slightest hint of water, and the only vegetation was the scraggly brush poking through cracks in the hard ground and the occasional tumble weed. Although I got an odd feeling the tumble weeds were more sentient than our plant life back home.

And then I turned.

To my left stood a lush forest, divided from the red desert as if a surveyor had marked a precise and geometrically defined border beyond which no deciduous life could pass. I walked over to the woods, shoving my arm through the invisible line to touch the bark of what looked to be a black locust sapling.

The magic flowed over my skin like cool spring water, like the sound of wind chimes in a lilac-scented breeze. My elven half sang at the feeling. I walked all the way in, breathing in the greenness of it all. This was Wythyn, the elven kingdom of my mother. And as much as I wanted to hate it as well as the elves who'd killed her, I couldn't help but be enchanted by the rich beauty of this forest.

But I wasn't here to marvel at the elven magic that had created such a Garden of Eden in a world of desert and swamp. I was here to see if I could mimic this skill. Or at the very least provide genetically modified crops that would somehow manage to thrive in the barren red clay and sand. Both seemed impossible tasks, even for a half-elf.

I left the lush forest and instantly sweated as the heat of the demon lands hit me once again. Ahead to my right was a different landscape, somewhere in between the two opposites I'd just experienced. The human area of Libertytown had been carved out of the elven forest, grudgingly 'gifted' to the humans after an imp named Sam, the Ha-Satan, had secured their freedom. Unfortunately, once that section of land was no longer part of the Elven Kingdoms, the elves had refused to continue the magical environmental controls that kept the land lush and fertile.

Thus Libertytown was fading like the fields in late autumn, trees bare of all but brown and yellow leaves, grasses baked in the sun, crops stunted and withering. I strode with purpose to the border, my shirt already clinging to my back with sweat.

The magic that hit my skin this time was faded and dull.

The air was dry, but without the intense heat of the demon lands. If this was what I had to work with, if the temperature and scant humidity were consistent, then there were crop modifications I could make that would feed these people. But I feared this was a mid-state, a stage on the slow slide into the inferno that lay just outside the border.

Somehow I had to make this work. I'd need to perform a miracle so Sam and her Archangel lover would grant immunity to Irix. He'd be able to walk among the humans without fear of an angel catching and killing him. He wouldn't have to keep dashing back to Hel to throw off the scent, waiting for the search to be over before coming back. I needed to do this for him. Somehow.

Plus, I did feel sorry for the humans here. They'd been kidnapped and brought to Hel, some as older children and adults, some as changeling babies. They were free now, but this was the only life they knew. If I couldn't help them, they'd have no choice but to return home through the gates, and try to carve out a life in a place where they didn't speak the language, had no marketable skills, and didn't even have basic identification. No one would believe hundreds of children who'd gone missing decades ago had suddenly turned up wearing strange clothes and speaking gibberish. And the changelings – their parents had buried the dead elven babies that had replaced them, thinking their children had stopped breathing in the night. As far as the human world was concerned, they were dead.

I ached for their plight, so here I was. Because of Irix, and because deep in my heart I wanted to help these people. But if I were to be completely honest with myself, there was another reason I was here – curiosity. I was a botanist, my shiny, newly printed degree hanging on the wall in my room back home. I'd thrown my cap in the air at graduation, thrilled to be starting a new life. And this was exactly the sort of challenge I loved.

"You *do* look like an elf!"

I spun around, my heart ready to pound out of my ribcage. Behind me was a small demon. He had long, lavender-colored limbs, and tiny scales on his torso along with tufts of hair sprouting from the top of his head and out of his ears. Instead of a nose, the demon had a long, wrinkly snout that twitched up and down. It made him look like a half-starved, perverted, Snuffleupagus.

"Are you…you must be Rutter?"

"In the flesh." The demon bowed. His odd appearance didn't bother me; I was just glad to meet someone this side of the gates who spoke English. As skilled as I was in botany, I sucked at foreign languages. I only knew a few phrases of heavily accented Elvish, and not one word of that weird language the demons and angels spoke. Rutter was assigned to me as an interpreter and a bodyguard. From his appearance I was thinking his skills in the former far outweighed his skills in the latter, although I hated to judge a demon by his color…and snout.

"So what's your plan, pretty elf-lady?" he asked. He was rubbing his snout and I wasn't sure if it was a suggestive motion, or he just had an itch.

"Walk into Libertytown. Talk to this mage Kirby. See if I can modify any existing crops to thrive in this environment. Depending on my success at that either go home or try to come up with another idea."

His face wrinkled upward. "Aren't you going to make the forests grow again? Like the elves did?"

"I'm a half-elf. Anything I do weather-wise or with the environmental conditions is going to have a very small radius and last for probably two hours tops. That's not a solution I can offer them,"

My words were rather abrupt and I immediately regretted snapping at the little guy. My shirt was glued to my body with sweat. My hair was a hot, limp mess down my back. I'm sure my eyeliner was raccoon-worthy. Still, that wasn't an excuse for being short-tempered with my demon escort.

He didn't seem to mind. I remembered hearing that he was a Low, the bottom-of-the-barrel as far as demon hierarchy went. Maybe he was used to being snapped at. Which made me feel even worse about my slip of temper.

"Well, I'm yours for however long you're here, so come with me, Miss Amber."

Rutter strode forward and I followed, easily keeping pace with his short, bowed legs. We left the blisteringly hot desert behind and entered into something that felt like a dry heat wave in a California summer. I reached out a hand to brush against the golden-green grasses and didn't recognize the strain, although they were similar to winter wheat back home. Hmm. Perhaps with some tweaking, I could get this to thrive in a more arid environment, although not in the desert I'd just walked out of. If that was what Libertytown was reverting to, I didn't have a lot of faith in my ability to hold their starvation in check for more than a year or two.

It was the same with the trees. Perhaps an Acacia would do better than these oaks and maples. I'd need to check the soil, since Acacia varieties didn't tolerate high levels of salt, and I doubted the human settlement had spare water for wide-scale leaching. They were very drought tolerant, though. And if the nighttime temps dropped low, Acacia did as well in cold as it did in heat. If evening temperatures didn't drop much below freezing, then possibly some Sumac – Rhus Iancea specifically - would thrive. They did well in the arid lands of South Africa, so there's nothing that said a similar species wouldn't do equally as well here.

Eucalyptus perhaps? Or Mesquites, which did so very well in poor soil.

Of course, none of this addressed the problem of crops. The humans could hardly eat Eucalyptus leaves like a koala. Alfalfa? Beans? Eggplant? Dwarf kale. Brassicas did well in hot, dry climates. I'd need to select a suitable cultivar, but even with a heat and drought-tolerant strain, we'd need to consider irrigation. There had to be a way to divert water here, and with even a small irrigation system, they could keep their soil stable enough to grow specialized crops.

"Rutter? Is there a water source nearby? A lake, or river, or even an underground spring?"

The demon turned to me his snout swinging with the motion. "The swamps aren't far. Rivers and lakes are mainly north and west."

Swamps. "How far are the swamps? Do you know what the water is like? Would it be suitable for irrigation, or even for humans to drink?"

He rubbed the side of his snout. "We can get to the swamps on foot in an hour or two. Do you want to go there? I thought you wanted to go see the humans and the Kirby Mage. I've never met an elf who liked the swamps, but since you're half demon, maybe you'll enjoy them."

"Can you describe them?" I pressed. I hated to take the time to truck out to these things if they were full of sulfur or had a PH that would etch metal.

"They're kind of gooey. There's green and blue slimy stuff on top, and sometimes your feet get stuck on the bottom and you drown. And the bitey fish – they're on you in seconds. The Mistress likes to eat them, but most demons think they taste like a bitter twig. They're kind of crunchy inside though, if you like that sort of thing."

"Do you drink the water?" He had to know more, but

getting information from Rutter was clearly an exercise in patience. "Do you think the humans could drink it?"

Rutter scrunched up his face, the snout shortening by a good six inches. "Drink it? Are you crazy? It's slimy. I've never seen anyone drink it. Well, maybe on a dare but that demon didn't look too good afterward,"

That answered my question. I still didn't want to give up on the idea of irrigation, but it seemed that endeavor might be a long-term project. I wasn't an engineer. Maybe if I put the wheels in motion, one of the humans here could take on the task of putting an irrigation system in place that drew water from the distant lakes.

Any further thoughts of crops receded to the back of my mind the moment the town came into sight. I'd expected something primitive, like grass-topped huts and crude stick fences, but what I saw would have put a European village to shame. The streets were cobblestone, smooth and even with a sandy mortar holding the stone together. Flanking the roads were row upon row of tall houses. Some were stone, some were brick, some were wood. A few had been done in a Tudor style with cedar wood batons and stucco over the wood framing. Straw and carved wood baskets sat outside colorfully painted doorways. I saw curtains in the windows, lacy with a floral or striped print. I also saw hundreds of eyes peering at me. A group of women stood in the street holding baskets of laundry. Their conversation died as they caught sight of me, and they watched silently as Rutter and I passed by.

I'd never felt so out of place. I'd been raised a human, completely unaware of my freakish genetic make-up until I was in college. I'd been an elven baby swapped for a human changeling one, except I wasn't dead, and I wasn't fully an elf. My mother, knowing how I would be hunted, had paid to have me declared dead and smuggled into the human world, to be raised as one of them. She'd had someone watch over me as I grew up. And she'd paid for her crime with her life. She'd intentionally lain with a demon, allowed one to impregnate her, and safeguarded the abomination that resulted from that union. Me. My whole childhood I'd been raised as Amber Lowry, while the real Amber had been stolen from her crib and served the elves in Hel as a slave until she'd been ransomed and brought home.

She was my sister, now called Nyalla. She was no blood relation to me. None of my human family was, but they were as close to me as any real siblings and parent could be. Nothing about me was human, but somewhere deep in my soul, I was. I'd always be a human. And the suspicion of these people I considered my own, their silence and staring eyes, cut me. They only saw an oddly dressed elf-woman with a demon escort. They only saw an elf, the same as all the elves that had enslaved them their entire lives. In their eyes I was no different, and I ached to think I'd been lumped in with a group of beings I'd grown to despise.

Rutter led me to a beautiful stone shop. It was three stories, and I assumed there were living quarters above the store. The heavy metal-reinforced wooden door made a cheerful jingle as he opened it and I walked into a paradise. The scent of cedar and cinnamon, of sage and lavender, of rue and juniper, all mixed with an acrid note of a sulfur match recently struck. Dried herbs hung from twine stretched along the ceiling. Stacks of staffs and wands were in a far corner. Each wall was lined with shelves packed full of labeled glass jars. But this was clearly a supply shop. I'd expected this Kirby person to have hundreds of finished goods for sale – amulets and scrolls, rune-covered wands and stones that glowed. There were a few baskets of stones behind a glass case, but none of them glowed. As much as I adored this shop, I was a bit let down. This wasn't any different than the occult and magical supply shops that I haunted back home. I'd expected…more.

A man came from a back room wiping his hands on his dark blue robe. He looked to be late twenties or early thirties with a shock of brown hair and an angular face. He wasn't much taller than I was, with a thin build that said he spent more time doing work that required fine motor skills instead of heavy labor. He greeted us in a language that sounded a lot like the Elvish Nyalla spoke when she'd first arrived. Then his eyes slid from Rutter to me and widened in shock before he dropped his gaze to the floor in front of my feet.

The words were still in Elvish, but from his posture and the cadence, I guessed he mistook me for some sort of Elven royalty. Then he looked a few feet up at my sneakers, my jeans, my Lord of the Rings t-shirt.

"You must be the botany expert that the Iblis sent." These words were in perfect English, as if he'd lived his entire life in some mid-western town.

"Amber Lowry." I walked forward and extended my hand. He hesitated, forcing his eyes up to my face and taking my hand.

"I'm Kirby. Mage Kirby. You're…young. And I didn't expect you to look so much like an elf."

Back home I took on the appearance of someone who was one hundred percent human. I'm not sure if it was a self-preservation thing on the part of my demon half, or just me being a chameleon. Hel was the only place where I seemed to change appearance, although I had no conscious control over it. Full demons could change their race and gender at will, but back home I always looked the same. I assumed that here, I'd always look like a high-born elven woman.

"It's…a sort of accommodation. Will I be staying here or somewhere else? Who is coordinating this project? I'm assuming there is a human liaison that I'll be working with while I'm here."

Kirby just stared at me a moment, his eyes glazed over. Then he shook his head and touched an amulet that hung around his neck. "I have a room for you upstairs. It's not fancy. I'm sure it's not what you're used to. I'm sorry."

I laughed. "I've been living in a dorm room for four years with cement block walls and metal frame bunk beds. I'm sure the room you have is more than suitable. Now…the project?"

He flushed red. What was going on? This guy was a mage, a talented and respected practitioner. He was also at least five years my senior. But here he was acting as if he were a bumbling teenager and I were Mrs. Robinson.

Oh. Half succubus. No wonder he was flustered.

"Where am I staying?" Rutter chimed in. He was pulling glass jars off the shelves and sniffing herbs. "In the room with Miss Amber? I want to stay with Miss Amber. I know she's a half-succubus, but she looks like an elf lady. She smells like one too."

I hesitated. Normally I wouldn't care if Rutter shacked up with me, as long as he didn't snore, but I'd probably need to be getting some mattress action in while here, and the little demon's presence would hinder any sexual activity. Although I wasn't sure having sex in a room with Kirby right next door or down the hall was a good idea. I'd might need to find somewhere else to work my mojo.

The thought put a knot in my stomach – working my mojo that is, not having to do it in a forest or an abandoned mill. If I were to help this community I'd need energy. Which meant I'd need sex. But who in all of Hel was I supposed to have sex with? Were there single, reasonably aged humans here who would be willing? The thought of having sex with demons scared me. Irix had always told me sex demons were at a disadvantage when it came to offensive and defensive capabilities as compared to other demons. I'd need to use my pheromones, or sweet talk my way out of any scary situation. And if they found out I was half-elf…no, demons were off the table. Elves? Equally problematic. Hopefully this town was filled with humans – humans that wouldn't compromise my ethics. I wasn't about to be the one who broke up a marriage, robbed the cradle, or sent Grandpa to an early grave.

And no socks with sandals. A girl had to have standards.

"You can shack up with me, Rutter. But not in my bed, okay?"

He saluted. "Got it."

Kirby looked relieved that he didn't have to arrange accommodations for the demon. "Are you tired? Or do you want to get started?"

"Get started." I was so fired up about this. "Rutter can you take my bag upstairs?" I'd packed a few clothes and some toiletries, not sure what would be available to me here, but I had another reason for getting Rutter out of the room. I needed to talk to Kirby.

I watched Rutter climb the back stairs then turned to the mage. "I know I look like an elf, but I'm only half-elf. I'm going to be doing a lot of genetic modification on crops and trees, and for that I'll need more energy than I currently have."

Kirby stared at me, perplexed. I waited, hoping he'd catch on. I got the idea that Kirby was kind of prudish and I didn't exactly want to come out and ask him to provide a list of willing sexual partners of an appropriate age.

Sure enough, he finally put the pieces together and realized what I was talking about. His face turned beet red, and again he touched the amulet around his neck. "I can ask, but I don't think we'll be able to accommodate your…needs. The humans here were all enslaved by elves. I doubt if any of them will be eager to have intimate contact with one. Unless…can you change form like the demons do? Maybe if you appeared human…"

"The other side of the gates I look human, but here elf is all I can seem to manage," I confessed. This was going to be a problem. If none of the humans would have sex with me, I'd need to consider demons – and I really didn't want to consider demons.

"I'll ask around," Kirby repeated. Again he touched the amulet around his neck, his hands shaking slightly.

"I assume that's to protect yourself against me." I pointed to it. "You don't need to worry. I don't seduce unwilling people. I won't entrance you and make you have sex with me."

"It's not…I don't want you to know my fantasies."

I did have a rather embarrassing habit of sensing the fantasies of those I met. It was a rude, prying thing to do, but I couldn't seem to help myself. The succubus in me was always on the prowl for a potential partner, and sensing someone's deepest desires helped that part of me decide whether I could satisfy them or not.

"I'm sorry. And yes, I probably would sense your fantasies. If it's any consolation, I've sensed some pretty freaky stuff in the last year. I mean, really freaky stuff." I'd done most of that freaky stuff, too. I'd not been sexually repressed when I thought I was a human, but my late-teen explorations were nothing compared to the things I found myself doing – and enjoying – as a half-succubus.

"This isn't freaky. I just don't want anyone to know."

He wasn't the only one with embarrassing fantasies, but I wasn't going to push him into revealing something he didn't want me to know about. Time to get back to the project. I'd worry about where the heck I was going to get enough energy to do all this later.

"I checked out some of your crops and trees on the way in and I have ideas for drought and heat-resistant alternatives. The big questions are how fast is the climate going to change, what's the end state, and do you know anything about the soil?"

Kirby blinked, his shoulders relaxing with the change in topic. "It's soil. That's about all I know. I'll have you meet with a group of the farmers, then afterward I have the crop records for you to peruse. The farmers should be able to answer any of your questions. Rutter will need to interpret since most of the humans here speak only Elvish, and I was told you didn't?"

He sounded incredulous that someone could look like me and *not* speak Elvish. "I don't. Will you be coming with us?"

He shook his head. "Not this time. I've got some orders I need to work on. Have Rutter bring you back when you're done and you can check the records. After that, we can discuss preliminary plans, as well as what resources you might need."

Sounded great to me. I rubbed my hands together, unable to keep from grinning with enthusiasm at the thought of starting this interesting and challenging project.

"Then let's get started."

CHAPTER 2

The farmers were helpful in that they knew the challenges of the soil, particularly the changing Ph. They also had dire news about the slow decline of the artificial climate controls. I'd been thinking of plants and trees that would thrive in southern Nevada, or New Mexico, when I should have been thinking of the Sahara Desert. The whole place was reverting to the demon lands just outside the fading barrier. Within the next few years, the soil would be acidic and filled with iron, the temperatures would swing sixty to eighty degrees from day to night, and the air would be dry as dust.

My heart ached. I could give them immediate relief, but even the modified crop production would dwindle and they'd be starving in two years. I needed to find edible plants suitable to the landscape here – crops that were indigenous to Hel. I wasn't sure that even those crops would sustain a human community like Libertytown, but it was a start. What had seemed a challenging project at the onset had now become an ongoing one where I came back every six months or so to check how the plants adjusted to the changing conditions, and tweaking where I could.

I knew it was temporary, but it was the best I could do. Hopefully in a few years, if the situation had deteriorated beyond what I could do to help, the humans would finally be convinced to leave.

It was late afternoon by the time Rutter led me back to the magic shop. The mage was bagging a mixture of herbs, a row of wands on the counter beside him.

"So, what do you think?" Kirby looked up at me with a quick smile before continuing to concentrate on the herbs. He seemed more at ease around me than he'd been previously.

"I think you should move," I told him, only half joking. "If not out of Hel, then somewhere besides Libertytown. The elves are leaving Hel. Maybe you can take over one of their kingdoms."

"It would be a short-term stopgap. Without the high elves here to maintain environmental conditions, the kingdoms will eventually revert to the normal landscape of Hel. I'd hate to uproot everyone for a few extra years of sustainable agriculture only to be right back where we are now. Besides, not all the elves are leaving. There are a few groups in each kingdom who have elected to remain. I'm sure they wouldn't appreciate us looting their homelands."

"But aren't the remaining elves going to be in the same situation as you? If the high elves are gone, who will maintain the artificial environment?"

Kirby shrugged. "I think they have some minor skills. The kingdoms might not be as lush as they are now, or the residents might be reducing the area of effect. Either way, I don't want to run the risk of elves finding us trespassing on their property. They're very territorial, and most of them blame the decline of their society on us. Well, mostly they blame the Iblis, but they also blame us."

Strike one. "I can do some crop modification, but nothing I know of is going to survive what Libertytown is eventually going to become. There has to be some indigenous plant life in Hel I can replicate. What do the demons eat? They must grow some kinds of crops, have livestock."

Kirby burst out laughing. Even Rutter joined in.

"Oh, Miss Amber. You are so funny! Demons don't grow plants," Rutter told me.

"They don't," Kirby confirmed. "They like to mooch off of the elves and dwarves, but mostly they eat whatever they come across. Most of those plants and animals would be poisonous to humans, or at the very least not nutritional."

Strike Two. Maybe. From what Kirby had said, I doubted that the humans could mooch off of the elves, but dwarves? I'd forgotten there were other races here.

"What do the dwarves eat? Maybe I could use some of their plants from this area. Or perhaps you could trade other skills and merchandise to them for food."

The mage looked up from his herbs, a puzzled expression on his face. "They mostly live in the mountains, so the climate is a bit different, but there are dwarves in the swamps and in the desolate lands. I doubt they import all their food. There must be something they eat."

Jackpot. Well, maybe not jackpot but possibly a solid lead. If I could get a good read on these plants, I could modify the ones the farmers were using, or even bring back specimens to replicate here.

"Is there any way you can put me in touch with a dwarf? Someone nearby I can talk with about these plants and their agriculture?"

Kirby pondered my questions a moment. "There's an old dwarf out in the swamps who has been there forever. She's the closest one I can think of that might be able to help." The mage looked over to Rutter. "She's a bit unconventional. I have a dwarf client coming by tomorrow. I'll ask him to take you to see her and make the introductions."

A glimmer of hope. Maybe I could cobble together a solution for these people after all. And there was one other possible solution I wanted to throw out there.

"What about purchasing all of your food? I realize that puts all the residents of Libertytown in a position of relying upon another group for food, but if a decent trade contract can be put together, you should be able to stockpile food for emergencies."

Kirby considered my idea. "That would be a last resort. There are groups here who would be happy to take advantage of that situation. We might be supplying them with luxury goods and services, but they'd have our lives in their hands. I don't feel comfortable about the balance of power in that sort of arrangement."

I understood, but these contracts didn't have to be with the elves or the demons. Sam had joked about having Peapod deliveries to Hel, but I didn't think that idea was too farfetched. The humans in Hel had much to offer, and an enterprising human the other side of the gates might be willing to provide a shipping container full of shelf-stable foods as well as fresh meat and produce in exchange. I pondered how I could broker such a thing, and decided that would have to wait until I returned home. It was becoming clear that I'd need to come back on a regular basis. I could scout out possible intra-gateway trade and propose it when I returned.

Kirby settled me in back room with a table and a chair, and a gigantic leather-bound book. After fidgeting for nearly an hour, Rutter snuck off to go "explore", leaving me in the shop with Kirby. I could hear the mage walking around the front room where the shop was located. Every now and then there would be a thump of something heavy, or a scraping noise. Had he been here all day long? Did he work twenty-four seven? I was beginning to think this mage had no life outside of his magic.

The book was the most depressing thing I'd ever read. Within months after taking possession of the area from the elves, the humans had begun to note a trend of increasing temperature and a drop in rainfall. I read the long list of numbers, looked over the charts, noted the correlations and predictive statistics. As I thought, the area had nine months to a year before their little sanctuary would be indistinguishable from the desert. The logs on crop production were equally disheartening. Survival rate of plants had plunged, even with the humans limiting the varieties to the more drought and heat-tolerant varieties. It was dark by the time I closed the book. I'd grabbed some crackers and something that looked like beef jerky from a cabinet, wondering if Kirby ever ate dinner.

Stretching, I made my way back to the front of the building, thinking I might just head to bed early and dive back into this in the morning. The mage was still in his shop, polishing stones by lamplight, a set of carving tools to his left. "Do you ever rest?" I teased. "Go party? Run naked through the woods? Kiss a girl? Eat dinner?"

He looked up to give me a quick smile. "This is my life. Most mages are infant changelings. I fell through the elven trap at ten years old. I've had to work twice as hard to make up for lost time."

I tilted my head, looking at him intently. "All magic, all the time. I know you've returned to see your parents. Isn't there anything else in your life? A girl the other side of the gates? A girl here? A passion for dominoes or a good smoked porter?"

He shook his head. "All magic, all the time. I see my parents once a month. I don't really have time for dating, or dominos, or smoked porter, whatever that is."

It seemed kind of sad, but maybe this was his passion, and magic was a jealous mistress?

"I'm not a virgin," he told me out of the blue. "There were a few girls when I was in academy, but just casual, you know. I don't have time...just no time for anything else."

I'd met the occasional asexual person. He didn't have to rationalize his feelings to me, but I got the impression there was more behind his hasty explanation. He'd not wanted me to know his fantasies, and his abrupt announcement made me even more curious what they were and why he was so desperate to hide them – and desperate to make sure I knew he had some sexual experience. Did he want to have sex with goats or something? I wouldn't judge, but that wasn't exactly something I could help him with.

"You don't want *me* to see your fantasies, is it possible that you don't want to see them yourself?"

He stared at the stone in his hand, rolling it around his palm. "Hardly. I've had them in my mind for most of my life. They'll never be realized. My fantasies are of something that will never come to pass. Doesn't mean I don't see them every night."

This was exactly the sort of man I went for back home. They desperately wanted something that they would never have in real life. I gave that to them. I gave them the impossible. And sharing their energy with me for the rest of their lives was a small price to pay for the realization of their sexual dreams. But I couldn't help Kirby if he didn't want to have those fantasies come to life.

"If you ever decide you want my help, let me know. I'm game for anything – as long as it doesn't involve killing or socks and sandals." Or animals, because I couldn't exactly transform myself into a goat.

He finally looked up at me, setting the stone back in the box. "You can't, though. You'll never be her. If it was just something kinky, I would probably fall right into your arms, but my fantasies are about someone in particular."

Ah, a long lost love. "No, I can't be that person. But I can play the part. If you have a need for closure, or want those fantasies you dream about every night to manifest I'll oblige. Sometimes an imitation can be just as satisfying as the real thing."

He shook his head and touched the amulet around his neck. "I can't."

I'd thrown it out there. If he wasn't willing, I wasn't going to press it. "I did some minor modifications to your plants in the field. The genetic modification will hold true to future crops, unlike most hybrids, but let me know if you begin to see a reduced harvest. I'll see what the dwarf lady has to say, and hopefully I can get you a few alternative crops. In six months or so I'll come back and see what else I can do to help."

He smiled. "Thanks, although I'm not sure what else you can do. I know we should leave. We probably will if the high elves don't come back. It's hard. For most of us Hel is the only home we know. And for me…magic is all I have. What would I do outside of Hel, deliver pizzas for a living?"

"I think you're underestimating yourself. My sister, Nyalla, was my changeling. She was a slave in Hel from infancy until she was almost nineteen. It wasn't easy for her, but she's carved out a life for herself. She's happy. And some magic does work on the other side of the gates. Someone with your skills wouldn't be delivering pizzas."

He sighed. "Maybe. I think everyone just needs time to

see if we can make this work. And if we can't, time to reconcile themselves to what we need to do."

I nodded and turned to leave. "You know how to reach me. I mean it – if you need me to come back before six months, let me know. I feel bad leaving you all with just some roots and a few other plants to feed a whole town full of people. So please let me know if you need me to come back and help."

I made my way back to the room with the book, pulling some dehydrated vegetables from another cupboard and stuffing a few in my mouth. They were sort of like bland, salt-free potato chips. Not great, but they'd satisfy my hunger. Not that they'd satisfy my other hunger. The work I'd done out in the field today had me drained and tired. I wouldn't be able to do much more without additional energy, but Kirby was right – none of the humans I'd met today would remotely consider sex with someone who looked like an elf.

"Amber?"

I turned around to see that Kirby had come into the room, a determined look in his eyes.

"I think...I mean, I know you need more energy. And maybe...you won't laugh?"

As if I would ever laugh at someone's fantasies. I reached out to touch Kirby's arm, and sensed something – something I hadn't felt from him before. I looked at his neck, at the collar of his robe and saw that the amulet wasn't there.

CHAPTER 3

"*Y*ou took it off? Kirby, are you sure? I don't want you to regret sharing with me. And showing me your fantasies doesn't mean you are obligated to let me fulfill them. It's always your decision. Always."

He took a deep breath, then let it out. "I...yes. I want what you have to offer. I mean, if you still want to. Because if you don't, that's fine. I'll understand."

Sheesh, this poor guy. What did he want that embarrassed him so? "The offer is always open, Kirby, as long as it's something I'm actually able to fulfill. I won't read you, though. You need to reach out to me. You need to show me, if you really want this."

He closed his eyes and visions flooded my mind – Kirby's fantasies. I slowed my breathing, struggling to control my impulses. "Do you…do you want this? I'm probably going to be here for a few days, then back regularly in the future. I'm not her. I can play the part, but will you be able to work with me afterward and see that I'm Amber? Can you separate me from the fantasy?"

"Yes. I mean, you don't look like her, not really. At first, there was a resemblance, but now that I know you I see you as Amber. I don't know if you can do it. I don't know if you really can fulfil this fantasy or not, but I want to try."

Fair enough. I just needed to make something very clear. "I can't be the real thing. I can only be an imitation. Is that something you want?"

"Yes. It's all I'll ever have, and it's better than nothing. I know what I said before. I…changed my mind. You need the energy, and in all honesty, if I'm going to have a succubus or an incubus fulfill my fantasies, I want it to be you and not some full demon that can't even assume a convincing elven form."

He just stood there as I lifted my hand to his cheek. The details of his fantasies took shape in my mind and I realized exactly why Kirby had kept this locked away, why he'd taken such care to craft and wear the amulet.

"Do you know what I want? Do you?" His face grew warm under my fingers, his gaze sliding away from mine. He was embarrassed. But there was no need for him to be embarrassed. We all had needs, and there was nothing shameful in what he desired.

Then I felt myself shimmer, change, just as I did when I crossed the gates. Kirby gasped. "Lady Aeoa. Amber, you look exactly like her right now. Exactly."

I more than looked like her, I was becoming her, falling into the role he needed me to play.

My fingers stroked along his jaw down to his chin. "I've watched you, Kirby. I'm very impressed by the progress you've made since you came here. Someday you'll be a sorcerer, one of the very few who hasn't been training since infancy."

He stood ramrod straight, his gaze focused respectfully

downward even though I held his chin. As emotionless and disciplined as his stance was, I could feel his breath hitch, his heart skip a beat. He'd lived for almost two decades craving this elven woman's notice, her recognition. He'd desperately wanted to stand out from the crowd of human mages in training. He'd wanted her praise. And he'd always wanted more.

Still holding his chin, I slid my thumb up to brush along his lower lip. "I've watched you, watched your hands as you carved wands and wondered what those hands would feel like on me. I've watched as you said the incantations, and wondered what my name would sound like on your lips in a moment of passion, what those lips would feel like on mine."

His heartbeat galloped, but all the while he kept his eyes downcast. He was just a lowly human, one mage among many. He couldn't ever approach an elven woman with such base desires. It would be up to the elf to seduce him. And that's exactly what I planned to do.

I released his chin and stepped back. For an instant, Kirby's gaze shot to mine, filled with longing and desperation before dropping downward again.

I took quick advantage and yanked the t-shirt over my head along with my bra, then shimmied out of my jeans and underwear. That was the one of two discordant notes in my portrayal of this fantasy – I hadn't had time to attire myself properly. Best to get naked as quickly as possible to keep the illusion alive. There was nothing I could do about my inability to speak Elvish, but at least I could ditch the human clothing.

"Look at me. Don't insult my beauty by averting your eyes. Look, and drink your fill of me." Kirby's eyes widened at the sight of the clothes on the floor, then his gaze slowly traveled up my body, taking in every inch of me.

When he'd halted at my chest, I took a step forward and

took his hand, placing it on one of my breasts. "These hands that work such magic. Let them work their magic on me."

He groaned, his fingers tightening an instant before they began to explore the soft skin, feeling the weight of my breast in his palm, then tracing the curve before brushing against my nipple. I stepped closer, angling my body so his erection rubbed the fabric of his cloak against me. Taking his other hand, I placed it on the small of my back, then leaned forward to place a gentle kiss on his lips.

"I know you won't disappoint me, Kirby," I murmured against his mouth. "All of your life, you've exceeded my every expectation. Kiss me. Worship me with your hands, with your mouth. Fill me."

He did as commanded, deepening the kiss. His fingers rolled my nipple, while his other hand shifted lower, caressing my backside. Reaching low, he pulled my hips against his before reaching between the back of my thighs to stroke my sex. It was an awkward position, my back arched at a crazy angle, but I needed to ensure he could touch all he wanted to touch.

He was hard as granite pushing the fabric of his robe against me. I worried this might be a fast ride for him. Kirby deserved so much more. He'd be fueling me with energy for the rest of his life, I wanted the fantasy that spurred our encounter to be slow and languorous, elegant and pristine. His desire for this elven woman went far beyond professional approval and sex. He'd seen her as an unobtainable goddess. When I'd told him to worship my body, I wasn't far off. For Kirby, this *was* an act of worship, it was the culmination of over two decades of reverence. For him, the joining of our bodies, the pleasure he gave and received, transcended the flesh. It allowed him to touch the one thing he'd always sought after in his magic – divinity.

I gave that to him. Our lovemaking was slow. Kirby

kissed and touched as though he were at a temple. As hard as he was, he held back, exploring every inch of my body, bringing me to orgasm all while he remained fully clothed.

Was this all he wanted? To give everything to this elven woman, to serve her without the hint of selfish release on his part? I searched his fantasy and saw that he wanted more, but didn't know how to proceed without turning something sacred into just regular sex.

I smiled benevolently, like a goddess bestowing a favor on her cherished pet. "Are you to deprive me of your manhood, Kirby? Deny me what I desire?"

His gaze dropped again, cheeks scarlet. "I can't. I can't do that to you. I can't."

"Then I will have to do that to you. Sit in the chair."

He took a step back and hesitated. My voice grew firm. "Kirby, sit. Sit and lift your robe so I may see you."

"Yes, my Lady," he stuttered. The mage backed up until I thought he would fall over the chair. Then he dropped into it, his hands shaking as he lifted the hem of the robe up to rest on his lap.

Sheesh. This poor guy must be in agony. I walked toward him with a sway of my hips, watching a pearl bead at the end of his cock. "You are to remain silent except for my name. Is that understood? I only want to hear my name."

He nodded, eyes still downcast. "Lady Aeoa."

"Lovely," I purred, reaching a finger out to stroke up his shaft. He jumped against my touch, his hands balled into tight fists at his side. Pausing a second, I gathered the drop on my finger and brought it up to my nipple. "You bring me gems, Kirby. Gems with which I can adorn myself."

His jaw clenched, his eyes lifting to stare once more at my breasts. Slowly I straddled him, my hands on the back of the chair on either side of his head. I lowered until he was lightly pressed against my opening, then I rocked my hips, letting him feel the soft wetness.

"Lady Aeoa," he gasped.

I eased downward, pausing every few inches to lift up before dropping further. Finally, my pelvis met his and I rested my weight lightly on him. "Kirby, put your hands around me, hold my hips. I want to feel your hands on me." He did and I leaned forward, kissing him, pulling his lower lip with my teeth before pulling away.

"Look at me Kirby. I need to see your eyes. I need to know that you live to serve me."

His gaze shot to mine and I began to move up and down, rocking my hips with each stroke. His fingers tightened on my rear and I let go of the chair, sitting upright and supporting my entire weight with the muscles of my thighs. My pace increased and I tightened the muscles in my pelvic floor, gripping him tight. His face was red, his fingers digging into my rear, but his eyes never left mine. I saw the struggle there, the desire to have this moment never end. Watching his eyes, I lifted my hands to my breasts and stroked my nipples. He shuddered, thickening inside me, but still he held back.

"I want you to come, Kirby. Give me your gift." I drove him deep inside, rocking my hips against him. He came, Lady Aeoa's name like a litany on his lips. And then he slumped against the chair, completely spent. I saw a tear at the edge of his closed eyelid and bent down to taste it, kissing him lightly on his forehead as I rose.

"Skilled in so many things," I murmured. "You please me, Kirby. As you have with everything you've done in your life, you please me."

Then I gathered my clothes from the floor and slipped out, automatically shifting back into my Amber appearance once I was in the hallway. Kirby never opened his eyes, the only thing moving was the rise and fall of his chest.

And that was how it should be. A goddess never stoops to retrieve fallen clothes, never slips out the door with wet trailing down her leg. A goddess just vanishes into the night, as a warm spring breeze, perfect in her divinity.

CHAPTER 4

I slept soundly, barely aware of Rutter coming into the room late at night and curling up in a lavender ball in an overstuffed chair. When I awoke, I felt like a new woman. I was humming with energy, ready to take on the world, ready to modify the genetic structure of hundreds of plants.

Rutter gave me a curious look, but didn't mention whether he noticed the difference in me or not. There was a basket of muffins outside my door and a bottle of milk, so the pair of us went downstairs and ate in the back room that seemed to serve as both a dining room and a horribly under-furnished kitchen. It was nice, sitting at the long wooden table with a purple-scaled, snouted demon devouring fruit and nut muffins and alternating swigs from the bottle of milk.

"Miss Amber?" Crumbs fell from the demon's mouth as he spoke. "What's it like the other side of the gates? I've never been."

I thought for a moment. "There are humans everywhere. In the cities, you can't walk down the street without seeing dozens if not hundreds of them. They use metal boxes on wheels to transport themselves at great speed – faster than an elf can run. And for long distances, they have metal flying devices that transport hundreds of humans."

Rutter took a drink of milk, wiping his lower lip with the side of his arm. "Are the humans nice? Do they like demons? Do they like Lows?"

"They don't know demons exist. The ones they meet are in human form and I guess they think of them as somewhat psychotic humans."

He sighed. "So I couldn't go there like this? I can't Own. I can't change my form. But I'd love to go see the humans and their world."

I thought about the panic Rutter would cause with his lavender scales and snout, but didn't have the heart to smash the little guy's dreams. "Maybe someday. Things are changing there. It's possible that soon you might be able to go there as you are and be accepted."

He crammed another muffin in his mouth. "I would like that. Would you guide me, Miss Amber? Would you show me how to drive the metal boxes and live in the cities?"

I envisioned myself playing tour guide to Rutter and couldn't help but smile. "Absolutely. When the time is right for you to cross the gates, I'll show you all the cool sites."

The Low grinned and nodded, his snout bouncing as he finished off the milk. I liked him. And I meant what I said. If he was ever able to cross the gates and walk around in his current form, I'd show him the Washington Monument, take him to the Smithsonian and the National Harbor. We'd have fun.

We were finishing up when I heard Kirby out in the shop. I wondered if things would be awkward between us. I tended to keep my succubus activity to partners I'd never see again with very few exceptions. This was kind of a peculiar circumstance, though.

I shouldn't have worried. Kirby acted as though last night had never happened, and I breathed a sigh of relief. Of course, part of his casual demeanor might have been because he had a customer.

He was a man that looked to be in his early thirties with a thick, curly, brown beard that looked softer than mink, and shoulder-length hair a shade lighter. He was about five feet tall and stood at one of the long tables, inspecting a row of wands.

A dwarf? I hated to assume. Back home this man would have been considered a shade on the tall side for an LP, but here in Hel I didn't know. Was he a human born with dwarfism, or a dwarf-dwarf?

"Andor, did you want another illusion scroll?" Kirby asked the man as Rutter translated for me. "I'm bagging the herbs you wanted right now, and I have the spelled gems in the back."

The man gave a polite nod. "Better make it two. Lart likes to have a back-up scroll on hand, just in case."

He hadn't looked at either me or Rutter. I stood there for a moment while Rutter went to paw through a basket of yarn. Kirby sealed up the bag of herbs, shooting me a quick, apologetic smile. "I'll be right back."

And now I was alone, standing right next to the man who hadn't glanced my way, hadn't acknowledged my presence. I was beginning to feel slighted. I know it sounds vain, but back home I was used to a certain amount of attention from others. At the very least a side-eye. This man acted as though I wasn't even in the room. Was it because I looked like an elf? Was the legendary rivalry between the two races a reality here in Hel?

"Hi," I blurted out unable to take the silence any longer.

"I'm Amber. This probably sounds rude, but are you a dwarf?"

Ugh. What a thing to say. Why had my charm, my manners, flown right out the window with this guy? The man looked at me in surprise. Rutter left the basket of yarn and jumped in to translate.

"I'm Andor Clawhammer of Clan Clawhammer. And yes, I am a dwarf."

His reply wasn't frosty or mean, but it wasn't warm either. The man's tone reminded me of someone on hold for nearly an hour, reciting his account number and current address to a call center representative.

And his reply was in English. A dwarf knew English. Other than Rutter and Kirby, he was the only one I'd encountered so far who had.

"Did Kirby speak with you about possibly accompanying me to see the dwarf lady in the swamps?"

He shot me a puzzled frown. "No."

I got the impression that he wasn't going to take me. Just in case the answer was 'no', I decided to see if *he* knew anything about dwarven agriculture.

"Does Clan Clawhammer live in the mountains or the swamps? Or in the desolate demon lands around Dis?"

A long silence followed my question. "Clan Clawhammer is a mountain clan, but several of us have spent a few centuries in the demon lands for business purposes."

Irix had said that dwarves acted as foster parents for groups of demon young, but this man didn't look like a childcare provider. Not in the least.

Andor turned his back to me, but I pressed on. "I'm here to help the humans develop crops and plant life that can thrive in the changing conditions of Libertytown. Without the elven environmental controls, the wheat and oats they are planting now won't be viable in another year. Already harvests are at a dangerously low level. I'm hoping to look at plants that dwarves use as food and perhaps replicate them here."

He shot me an odd look over his shoulder. "You're an elf who speaks a human language, and wants to help the humans. Why?"

"Because their other alternatives are death or crossing the gates to a world some of them left behind as infants. I want migration to be a last resort. I'm hoping they can manage to carve a life out here in Hel, just as the dwarves have."

Silence fell heavy in the room. I wasn't sure the dwarf would speak again, but was determined to keep my mouth shut and wait him out.

"The mountain plants might not thrive here, but the dwarf you asked to see, the one who lives in the swamp, knows the flora and fauna in this area better than most. She could tell you which plants are edible. Sometimes she demands a price."

My heart sank. Did this dwarven lady take Visa? Or maybe the three twenties I had in my back pocket? "What sort of price?"

Andor shrugged. "I don't know. That's for her to decide. If that's the reason you want to meet with her, I'll take you. I'm going past there on my way back."

For someone who seemed predisposed to dislike me, he was being very accommodating. I smiled and thanked him, thinking about what I might bring that would repay the woman for her information.

Kirby came back to the room, looking back and forth between us with a slight frown on his face. "Amber is here to help us turn around our crop failures. She's a half-elf/half-demon who was raised as a human the other side of the gates. I was going to ask if you'd escort her to visit the Oma in the swamp, so she can find out about some of the plants indigenous to this area."

Andor gave me a sharp nod and turned to face the mage. As dismissive as the gesture seemed, I got the feeling that Kirby's recommendation carried some weight with him. And I particularly noted that he didn't bat an eyelid at the mention of my half-breed status. That gave me some hope that he wouldn't sell me out to the elves or the demons the moment we'd left the city.

The dwarf completed his transactions with Kirby, and he, Rutter, and I headed out. The swamp lands were only an hour or two walk from Libertytown, and Rutter promised to have me back before nightfall.

After the first hour of walking, the red sand became dotted with coarse grasses. Eventually the grasses took over and a few stunted trees emerged. I could smell the sulfur from the swamps ahead, and as foul as the odor was, at least it signified water.

"Where do the swamps come from? I mean, I can see the landscape transition, but it seems abrupt for such a short distance. There must be something feeding into them."

Andor adjusted the pack on his shoulder, then glanced over at the pool. "The water is stagnant, so if they're spring fed, it's not significant. Change in Hel *is* abrupt – and not just climate and landscape. It's the demons. They are chaos incarnate."

The demons affected the environment? Just their presence, or was it intentional? We made our way around the marshy areas, Andor keeping us on the narrow path of solid ground between what looked like thick quicksand and fetid water. I smacked at the bugs the size of small birds that were determined to take a bite out of any exposed flesh. A small house appeared in the distance. It was stone with a tin roof, a curl of smoke coming from the chimney.

As we got nearer, I saw a carved staff by the door with a metal end.

"This is the Maugan Swamp," Andor told me. "And this house belongs to Oleana Clawhammer."

I could hear the reverence in his voice. The door opened and a woman stood on the threshold. Her red-brown face was heavily lined, with a broad nose and piercing gray eyes. Thick silver braids hung from either side of her head, almost brushing the ground. She wore a dark blue apron over a long, blue and white checked dress. Bare feet peeked out from beneath the hem. She spoke, and Rutter translated for me.

"Andor! It has been far too long since you've visited me."

My dwarven escort hustled forward to place a kiss on the thick silver ring that the woman wore on her thumb. "Oma, I have brought someone who requests the gift of knowledge."

He spoke to her in English. Were dwarves especially skilled in languages or did they have lots of contact with English-speaking humans? I had thought Rutter would need to translate for everyone I'd meet, but it seemed some of the residents of Hel *did* speak my language.

The woman peered at me, her scrutiny making me feel like a bug on a collector's board. "Is this your woman, Andor? I saw in the leaves that you would love outside of the dwarven race, but I didn't foretell this elf/succubus woman."

Andor looked appalled. "No, she is *not* my woman. Mage Kirby brought her through the gates from her human home to assist them in crop production."

She snorted. "More likely she's going to help them have an orgy. Come in, come in. Normally I'd chase this girl away with my staff, but I'm intrigued. And she *is* easy on the eyes."

"I'm honored to meet you Ms. Clawhammer," I said, bowing. "My name is Amber Lowry, and as Andor said, I'm here in Hel to help the humans develop sustainable agriculture in the changing climate of Libertytown. I'm hoping you can help me identify appropriate indigenous plants and perhaps point me to where I can obtain samples."

She waved me in, herding me toward a long wooden table with a series of doodles carved into the surface. I sat down into a straw-backed chair. There was another dwarf in the room – one that looked to be not much older than Andor but with golden blond hair and beard. The two male dwarves spoke, then the blond one walked over to Oleana and placed a loud kiss on her cheek. The elderly dwarf scowled, but the edge of her mouth curled into a smile as she smacked the dwarf on the ass with a spoon. Then she turned and stirred the contents of a stock pot with the same spoon while the two male dwarves left the house together.

"Are you hungry?"

What else did she use that spoon on before it went into the pot? Before I could politely decline, the dwarf woman set a bowl of hot soup in front of me and shoved a spoon into my hand. Rutter also got a bowl and went to sit in the corner to eat. I could hardly claim not to be hungry without offending her, so I blew on a spoonful of the soup and ate it.

Holy cow it was spicy. But good. Even though I was not particularly hungry and seriously concerned about the food sanitation practices in this kitchen, I still ate the soup. Tasty was tasty. I just didn't want to know what was in it or where exactly that spoon had been.

"Humans," the dwarf complained. "Always wanting to talk business before food. It's a rudeness I tolerate, assuming that a short lifespan means they need to rush everything. I expect better of you, half-elf. The humans in Libertytown won't starve to death in the next few hours. Eat your dinner, then we will talk."

I'm ashamed to admit that I cleaned the bowl, and even graciously accepted a second helping. Rutter got some meat jerky stuff after his soup and sat by my feet, gnawing on it while I slurped away. Once I was done, Oleana picked up the dishes and put them in a wash basin, then she sat down opposite me and folded her hands together.

"Roots are your best bet. Eight different varieties thrive in this acidic soil, but you'll need irrigation. Get used to no trees unless you can somehow bring enough water up from the ground to support them, too. I assume the priority is food, so you might want to forget about shade for the time being." She stood and pulled a box from under the counter, then disappeared through a back door. Seconds later she had returned, handing me the box. Inside were bunches of roots with the tops still attached. They looked similar to our parsnips and turnips, and I was willing to bet the leafy greens would be just as edible as the tubers. This would help, but the humans at Libertytown would need more variety than this for diet as well as crop rotation.

"How about any of the desert plants? I'm assuming not those tumbleweeds, but is anything else edible?"

She pursed her lips. "Some of the cactus down near Dis is edible, but it wouldn't be the best use of field space. Maybe they could use it as an ornamental, or along the edge of the planted fields."

"Thanks. How about a leafy green or a vegetable? Would something like zucchini or radicchio grow there? Grain?" I asked.

"The grasslands between the desert and the swamps don't have edible plant life. Up in the mountains we grow grains and vegetables with very little water, but the temperatures in Libertytown are already too high for those to survive. There is a thick-skinned fruit that grows on a succulent near Dis. It's like a pomegranate. Honestly, your biggest problems are the lack of water and the swings in temperature between day and night. The high elves modified the environment to a great degree, but small changes would go a long way toward making Libertytown sustainable for humans."

These roots might be all the humans could grow, and even then I would have to figure out a way to irrigate. Pomegranates were a possibility. And if I could somehow manage to bio-dome the fields to hold the heat in at night and filter the intense daytime sun, we might be able to do grains and vegetables from the mountains. I'd seen plastic sheeting used to protect against frost, keeping the heat from escaping sun-warmed ground during the nighttime hours. Even if they didn't have plastics here, I could convince Sam to send a few thousand rolls across the gates. That would take care of the evening temps, but I still needed to deal with the intense daytime heat and the lack of water.

"I might be able to use some human techniques from across the gates to stabilize the temperate. Combine that with some genetic modification, and it might be possible to get the drought-resistant mountain plants to survive."

The dwarf pursed her lips then nodded. "I'll have Andor escort you there and introduce you to Svetek. She'll give you some samples that you can take back."

I looked down at the box she'd just given me. "Can I pick this up on the way back?"

She smiled, the wrinkles on her cheeks creasing into deep lines. "I'll have someone deliver them to Libertytown. That way you don't need to carry them yourself."

"Thank you." Things were looking up. It wouldn't be an easy road for the humans here, but there seemed to be a dim light at the end of the long tunnel.

"You said we'd need to bring the water up for irrigation. I'm assuming there is a spring system that runs under the desert? How deep is the water table, and how can we divine where the lines run?"

Oleana chuckled. "Smart girl. Seems you've got more to

you than sex after all. Yes, there are underground streams, but they are far underground. In the area of Libertytown, I'd guess anywhere from three thousand to ten thousand feet below the surface. And, of course, that makes divining for their location difficult. I think there are some maps of the underground waterways that the elves commissioned. If you could get your hands on those, it might make water location easier."

It would, but then there would be the issue of drilling so far and pumping the water to the surface. Did anyone in Hel have the technology for that sort of thing? I'm sure they had basic wells, and maybe used magic for these purposes, but a ten thousand foot well was not something that could be accomplished with a flick of a wand, as far as I knew.

"Do you have any other suggestions?" I asked her.

"Have the humans leave Hel. The demons won't care if they starve. The elves won't care if they starve. They're on their own if they persist in trying to carve an independent existence here. It's going to be difficult. It might be easier to face the challenges of returning home."

I thanked her. As Rutter and I got up to leave she halted me with an outstretched hand. "Don't you wish to know your future, half-elf?"

My future. My long, tens of thousands of years' future. I'd watch the humans I loved die. I was despised by my mother's people, and viewed as a play toy by my sire's. Those were the constants of my future. The unknowns were whether Irix and I would spend it together, and that was one question I was terrified to know the answer to.

"No. I don't want to know my future. Thank you for the offer, though."

She chuckled. "Wise. My parting advice to you, then is to love with your heart, not just your body."

It was something I tried to do every day.

CHAPTER 5

Along with the sample root vegetables, Oleana also sent word to Kirby that we'd be gone longer than just the afternoon. When Andor initially informed me that it was a three day walk to the mountains, I'd hesitated. I'd planned to be in Hel only a few days, a week max. Six days back and forth to the mountains, plus another few days modifying plants and assisting with irrigation would cut it close. I had a much-anticipated internship in two weeks, so I couldn't stay here longer than planned.

I'd stood there outside of Oleana's house, biting my lip and wondering if I could make plans to come back in the fall and what my half-done project would mean to Irix's immunity. Andor was packing a large bag with foodstuff and water, and another with what looked like bedrolls. Just as I was about to tell him I couldn't go, he turned to me, his dark eyes intense as they took in my expression.

"If you're willing to move fast, we can do the journey in a little over a day. And I'll give you one of my elf buttons for the return trip." He looked over at Rutter and sighed. "Two of them."

Elf buttons? I looked down at my t-shirt and jeans, wondering what elf buttons were for. Maybe I was supposed to trade them to someone for a horse? Didn't seem like a fair trade to me, but I didn't know how such things worked in Hel.

"They're an elven-made transportation device that looks like a push-button. The ones I have will take you and your demon escort right outside of Patchine, which is only a few hours walk from LIbertytown."

He turned his back on me and continued packing. These elf buttons sounded expensive. I thought about the twenties I had in my pocket, about my Visa card. "How much do you want for them?"

"Nothing. I've collected quite a few of them over the last few centuries. Things like that are a better trade than the 'favors' demons like to offer. Besides, I won't be able to accompany you back and a half-elf girl with a Low will most likely be dead before you pass through the Gray-bridge Gap." He looked up at me briefly. "I promised Kirby you'd be back. I intend to make good on that promise."

"Thank you." I took the pack he handed me and slung it across my shoulders. Without another word, the three of us set out west through the swamps.

After a few hours, the swamps cleared and once again I faced an endless landscape of tall grass and the occasional gnarled tree. Off in the distance were gray shadows that I assumed were mountains. I really wanted to let Rutter take a turn carrying my pack, but Andor announced we were going to "jog" and I wasn't sure the Low could keep up with the two of us if he was carrying a pack. I eyed the dwarf with his short legs and pack of his own and wondered if Andor would even be able to keep up. I was an elf. I was fast, even if I had an additional twenty pounds on my back.

I needn't have worried. Andor took the lead with a

pounding, steady, surprisingly long stride. I could have easily outrun him, but after two hours of this pace I was feeling as if my legs were about to fall off. I was clearly the sprinter where the dwarf was the marathoner. Rutter was no slow-poke either, although he tended to dart off to look at interesting lizards or trees, then complain loudly when we wouldn't slow down for him to catch up. Night fell, and Andor kept going, never missing a step. What was he, Super Dwarf? Didn't the guy get tired? Hungry? Thirsty? I had excellent night-vision, but still I tripped over an unexpected rock and did a face-plant onto the ground, sliding forward in the dirt from my momentum.

Andor halted and watched me get up. I was glad it was dark because I was probably covered in dirt with road-rash on my hands and arms.

"We'll camp here."

More welcome words were never said. I collapsed where I stood and pulled the pack from my back, yanking out a blanket before tossing it over to the dwarf. I didn't care if I ate or drank, I just wanted to sleep.

Sleep proved elusive with my aching legs, and it was diffi-cult to find a place on the ground that wasn't littered with rocks. I sat up and watched Andor unpack a selection of meats, cheeses, bread, and fruits. My stomach rumbled and suddenly food was more important than sleep.

Rutter finally caught up with us, and I half listened to his chatter as I ate. Immediately after I'd finished my food, I was asleep on the rocky ground, dreaming that I was still running through the grasslands.

CHAPTER 6

"Shh."

I awoke with a start to a hand over my mouth and someone's arm pressing me into the ground. Andor. He took the hand away when he realized I wasn't going to scream and sat back on his heels.

Rutter wasn't in his blanket, and about twenty feet away was a loud rustling and rumbling noise. We were still lying down in the grass. Andor put a hand on my shoulder when I tried to rise and once again put his finger to his lips.

The rustling came closer, and now I heard a voice – voices actually. I couldn't understand what they were saying but they spoke in low guttural tones. The wind shifted and my eyes watered. Whoever it was they hadn't bathed in…well in forever. The closer they got, the harder it was to breathe. These things stank so badly that I was considering suffocation as a better alternative to their smell.

One came close and I froze, understanding why Andor had wanted us to remain undetected. They weren't human, and they didn't look friendly. The three creatures were close to seven feet tall with huge bulging muscles in yellowish skin. They were naked, and my eyes involuntarily drifted downward. I winced. Big. Like, rip-me-in-half big. And their sexual organs had jagged protuberances that didn't bode well for the survival of anyone on the receiving end. How the heck did they procreate? Were their women lined with iron? I might be a succubus, but even if they hadn't stunk, there's no way I'd be jumping in to fulfill their fantasies.

Each one carried a club with spikes imbedded at the end. They talked loudly between themselves, but must have had poor eyesight because they didn't once look our way. Hopefully their own powerful smell masked our own, and if we held very still, they wouldn't see us.

I didn't want to think what would happen if they did see us. Rutter was nowhere to be found and I wasn't sure what good he'd be against these things. I got the feeling Andor was handy to have around in a fight, but there were three of them and two of us, plus they had to have outweighed us by close to two thousand pounds.

I waited until I could no longer hear them, until their horrid smell had died to a more tolerable level before turning to Andor and raising my eyebrows.

"Ogres." He stood and walked back to his blanket. "Sunup is in an hour. Go back to sleep."

Right. Like I could sleep after that. "What would they have done if they'd seen us?" I whispered.

"Roasted us on a spit for dinner." The dwarf wrapped the blanket around himself and lay down. The conversation was obviously over.

My mind wouldn't give it a rest, though. Ogres. Like from the role-playing games I'd participated in? I imagined a fight between us – Andor with his axe, me able to not do much beyond shoot lightning bolts and grow the grass around us into a jungle. Normally I'd run, pretty sure I could easily outpace those big oafs, but my legs were sore and even as well as I saw in the dark, I'd probably trip within the first ten feet on these rocks hidden in the grasses.

Roasted on a spit. One more thing in Hel I needed to fear. Why the humans wanted to stay here was beyond me.

Rutter came back at sunup with a handful of squirming lizards. He kindly offered to share them, but I declined. Then he proceeded to sit down on his blanket and eat them one by one. They made a horrible crunching noise, their tails twitching until he slurped them down. It made me not want breakfast.

In the daylight, I clearly saw why I'd tripped and why I felt like the Princess and the Pea this morning. The mountains loomed before us, and the rocky ground sloped upward from the grassy plains. In less than a mile we'd be negotiating rocks and boulders, winding along switchbacks as we climbed. I wasn't sure if there was a mountain pass, or a tunnel from a cave that cut through, but either way the trip ahead was daunting.

"We made good time yesterday," Andor said. I hadn't heard him rise, but he already had his blanket packed and was munching on something that looked like a pear.

"Are we going to keep running?" I was pretty agile, and didn't think I'd suffer another fall with the light of day to guide me, but my legs were still killing me from yesterday's exercise.

The dwarf shook his head, tossing the pear core into the grasses. "There's a cave and an entrance to the pass-through about a mile from here at the foot of the mountains. Those caves interlock and connect with passages all through the mountains, some of them made by us, others naturally occurring. We should be in Vetil by late afternoon."

I did the math figuring a few hours to speak to the dwarves and collect some plants, then we could teleport to Patchine via elf button before nightfall. If we hurried, I could be back in Libertytown tonight. The thought put a spring in my step and I jumped up, packing my and Rutter's blankets and grabbing a piece of the fruit for the road. The little demon had finished his lizard breakfast and was doing an odd set of calisthenics. Andor slung his bag over his shoulder, and we were on our way.

The rocks were larger the closer we got to the mountains until they were well above the tall grass and we were forced to weave around them. The cave entrance was massive, and once inside I counted eight different tunnels. Andor took a gem from his pack and scraped it across the cave wall. It lit up like a lantern, casting a golden light. The tunnel was narrow with several branches to the right and left. Every so often we came into a larger underground room. Andor walked briskly, confidently through the labyrinth, so I was surprised when he came to an abrupt stop at the entrance to one of the large 'rooms'.

"Stay here." He dropped the stone onto the floor and with far more speed and stealth than I'd ever imagined a dwarf could have he was gone, leaving Rutter and me in the narrow tunnel. Ahead was darkness the like of which I'd never seen before. The little stone's faint light only illuminated the first few feet of what I assumed was a giant room. Rutter and I waited for what seemed like hours, until I began to fear our dwarven escort had ditched us.

We'd never get out of here. I had no idea which way would take us back outside and I was sure Rutter was equally clueless. We'd wander around these caves until we died of dehydration or starvation. Or until something ate us.

A memory of last night's ogres sprang to my mind just as I heard a noise in the room before us. It was a soft noise, like the brush of a hand against the stone walls. Rutter edged close to me and I held my breath.

Idiot. Andor had just told us to stay put, no doubt so we

wouldn't get lost while he…I don't know, scouted ahead or something. He'd even left us the light. There was nothing wrong, and the dwarf wouldn't abandon us. He'd promised Kirby, and I got the feeling he was a man of his word.

Again the soft brush of something against the stone, this time closer.

"Andor?" I whispered. There was no response so I edged my way into the room, staying within the light and squinting to get an idea of my surroundings.

I thought I could make out three tunnel entrances to my right, but straight ahead stretched beyond what my eyes could see in the darkness. I turned to step back and something grabbed me.

I shouted. Twisting to get free I felt long claws scratch down my arm, and the snap of teeth close to my ear.

"Get off Miss Amber, you lizard!" Rutter kicked the thing, then jumped on its back, punching with one fist. He was holding the light in the other hand, so I got a good look at what was trying to chew the side of my head. It was a giant lizard, up on two legs with slimy skin and bulging white eyes. Again it snapped at my face, ignoring the demon to focus its attentions on me.

I didn't know what to do, so I shot a lightning bolt at the thing. I felt the sizzle of the electricity run through the lizard, jolting me in the process since I was in contact with the creature. Rutter flew backwards. The lizard squealed and let go of me to drop onto all fours.

I was free, but this monster was between me and Rutter. I couldn't leave the Low and run blind and lost through the tunnels. My only option was to stay and fight it.

So that's what I did, crouching like a wrestler as I sized the thing up. Rutter had dropped the light, so I had a clear view. The lizard was gray with black spots and a skin that appeared wet and slippery. He was skinny, with long limbs. If

I could stay free of the teeth and the claws, I might be able to push enough electricity through it to kill it. Or I could just stay here and continue to shoot lightning at a safe distance. Yeah, that was the better choice.

Another lightning bolt hit it square in the chest, knocking it to the ground. With another squeal, it got up and charged.

"*Bally-mea!*" There was a sharp whistle followed by a few shouted words and the giant lizard pivoted mid run, dropping to all fours and running to greet Andor and two other dwarves. The female dwarf patted it on the head, then glared at me accusingly.

"Did you have to nearly cook our watch-lizard?" Andor asked.

Was he angry? Amused? It was so hard to tell with this dwarf.

"Yes. When I'm attacked by a giant lizard that scratches me and tries to bite my head, I tend to defend myself."

The dwarf lifted an eyebrow. "You came out of the tunnel. This room is his boundary. If you'd stayed in the tunnel like I told you, then you would have been fine."

I folded my arms across my chest. "I heard something moving around and literally took one step out of the tunnel. If you had told me a giant lizard would try to eat me, if you had told me how long you were going to be gone, maybe I would have heeded your instructions. Maybe next time introduce me to the watch-lizard so it doesn't attack me?"

The female dwarf was still glaring at me, caressing the slimy thing on the head. The other dwarf was gawking at me as if were an exotic zoo creature. Andor looked as if he was ambivalent to my nearly being eaten by a lizard. Rutter was against the wall in a heap.

Rutter! I raced over and gathered the Low up in my arms, trying to check his pulse. Did demons have pulses? Where was I supposed to check? His wrists? His neck? His snout?

Just as I put my fingers on the springy thing, Rutter's eyes flew open. He pushed the snout into my hand with a grin and I hastily dropped it.

"I thought you were dead. Or at the very least hurt," I exclaimed.

He turned to rub his snout against the side of my breast. "Only playing dead, Miss Amber. You had the situation under control. I would have helped if you'd needed it." Again he rubbed his snout on my breast, the fleshy tip stretching to do a reach-around to the front. "Can you do that with your fingers again? That was nice."

His fantasies flooded my mind and I resisted the urge to drop him on the floor and go find a shower. The demon side of me was intrigued, especially given our anatomical differences. The rest of me was thinking *there's no way that's going to happen.*

"Um, maybe another time Rutter. Okay?"

He sighed and got to his feet, dusting himself off. "No problem, Miss Amber. Succubi are picky. I know they'd never do the boinky-boink with a Low."

That broke my heart. Why wouldn't sex demons do the boinky-boink with Lows? Yes, the demon form and particularly that weird snout were off-putting to someone who'd grown up thinking she was a human, but the succubi and incubi here should be used to this sort of thing. Why *not* a Low? Rutter was sweet, and he'd jumped right on that lizard to save me. He might not be top of the stack when it came to the demon hierarchy here in Hel, but I'd bet the energy he'd transfer to me would be just as strong as any other demon. Maybe stronger. In my experience, it was the ones no one else wanted who gave me five times what the players did.

"I'm not like other succubi, Rutter. I don't care if you're a Low, it's just that I've got a lot I need to do in a short amount of time. And we *do* have an audience."

We did. The female was still petting the lizard, murmuring soothing words to it. The male still stared at me. Andor was watching the pair of us, a surprised expression on his face. Out of the three he was probably the only one who had understood my words. I felt my face heat up to realize he'd just heard me basically give a rain-check to the Low. One more reason for him to despise me, I guess.

"I'm sorry I hurt your lizard," I said, rising to my feet. "I'm assuming this is the entrance to your underground city?"

I'd expected him to lead us through the mountains to the other side where their farming most likely took place. Although they could have farming deep within the mountain using magical light sources and hydroponics, I didn't think those plant strains would be adaptable to the intense light, heat, and arid conditions of Libertytown. Hopefully this trip wouldn't be a complete waste of my time.

"I wasn't sure you'd be allowed inside, so I brought Mellok and Svetek to meet with you here. They can provide you with plant samples without needing to continue through the mountain for another day. I'm assuming harvested samples would be sufficient?"

Crap. Mellok and Svetek didn't look predisposed to help me out after I'd zapped their lizard. "Yes, samples will help as long as Libertytown can purchase clippings, seeds, or root-stock if needed."

He nodded. "Of course. Any plant that doesn't need your modifications is available for them to purchase, or for trade."

The woman turned to Andor and spoke. He replied, and after a moment of conversation, turned to me.

"Svetek said you can step inside the city gates. She has her staff preparing boxes of grains, fruits, vegetables, and leafy greens that might be suitable for Libertytown with slight modifications."

Rutter and I followed Andor and Svetek into the back

shadows of the cavern while Mellok remained behind with their guard lizard. The thing snarled at me as I passed, making me glad that the dwarves had it well trained. In the back of the cavern there was a giant set of metal doors with ornate embellishments across the lower half. I eyed them, wondering how much they weighed.

With a sweep of Andor's hand, the doors swung open revealing something out of a fairy tale. This cavern was huge, stretching hundreds of feet upward. Houses jutted from the walls, impossibly suspended into mid-air. There had to have been a thousand homes lining the walls, no doubt extending far back into the rock. Narrow stone paths connected them all. A woman with a metal-tipped staff was climbing the path toward us, a cart full of crates pulled by two small lizard creatures behind her.

"Here are your samples."

A cart. Full of crates. "How am I supposed to get this back to Libertytown? Does the elf button transport a cart and two lizards?"

"You touch the cart when you transport and it will go with you. Anything living requires a second button, which is why I'm providing one to your demon companion."

So no lizards. How the heck was I supposed to transport a cart once I got to Patchine? I envisioned Rutter and I hauling it through the desert. I guess that was my problem, though. Andor had gone out of his way to escort me here, provide me with samples and return transportation, protect me from ogres and watch-lizards. I'd just have to make do somehow. Maybe this Patchine place had horses? Or lizards? Or demons willing to haul a cart for a twenty?

Instead of pestering Andor for additional transportation help, I went to meet the cart, being careful to avoid the lizards with their sharp teeth. Carefully I examined the contents of each crate. The fruits were hearty, thick-skinned figs and pomegranates. There were cuttings for almonds and olives that would thrive with very little modification. There was even a variety of apple that I thought might yield a decent crop given the conditions. What really surprised me was the grain – thick, saw-edged grasses that had wheat-like seeds. I could tell the moment I lay my hands on them that they took very little water and were able to survive brutal temperature swings.

There were roughly a hundred samples of each – enough to get the humans started. I'd need to come back in a few months, maybe at the end of my internship at the vineyard, to adjust anything that wasn't at maximum output and to modify enough that they'd have a solid base planting stock. Roots from the swamps, wild cacti from the desert, fruit and grain from the mountains. The humans could trade for anything else. All I needed now was an irrigation system.

And for that I'd need to go to the elves.

CHAPTER 7

We arrived in the desert, a city about a mile off. Libertytown was a speck in the distance. The sun was golden-pink on the horizon, and I had a cart with no lizards. Or horses.

"Can we leave it here?" I asked Rutter. "We can send someone from Libertytown to retrieve it up in the morning."

He shook his head. "It will be picked clean. Or burned. If the sand wyrms don't get into it, a roving group of demons will."

I didn't go all the way to the mountains to have my supplies stolen, so I picked up one end of the wagon shaft, braced myself against the yoke, and pulled. Rutter did the same on the other side and slowly we moved the wagon forward. It was only a quarter mile to Patchine. Once there I could bribe some demons to help haul it to Libertytown in the dark. If they didn't take my cash, then hopefully Kirby could step in to compensate them.

We were moving at a painfully slow pace, due to the soft, sandy dirt, the weight of the wagon, and the fact that neither Rutter nor I were experienced at team pulling. I was sweaty and exhausted after we'd gone only thirty feet. The city seemed even farther away, and I caught sight of something moving closer – something that looked like a group of…creatures.

"Rutter? Who's coming towards us?"

Rutter looked up. "Demons. Three of them."

Should I run and hide and abandon my cart to potential looters? And hide where? There was nothing bigger than a tumbleweed nearby. Maybe I could crawl in the cart with the crates, although if the demons looted the wagon, I'd surely be found.

"What do I do?" I hissed. They were moving fast, no doubt running.

Rutter dropped the yoke leaving me with all the weight, and walked forward, standing partially in front of me. I appreciated the effort, but a small Low wasn't going to block me from view. What to do? How could I explain my presence here without making me more of an interesting object to haul home as a demon-toy?

"Tell them I'm an elf," I told Rutter. "A mute elf in human clothing, one who has taken a vow of silence in honor of the Goddess, and that you're escorting me somewhere."

The demon's eyes widened as he glanced back at me. "A Low? Escorting an elven lady?"

We didn't have time to argue further because the demon travelers were within earshot. I dropped my side of the yoke and stepped away from the shaft, well aware that an elven lady wouldn't be pulling a wagon. Then I raised my chin and tried to look aloof and imperious. What would a full-elf, one who actually lived in Hel, do in this circumstance? The demons hailed us and Rutter shouted something back. I looked, figuring I'd better at least see what I was up against.

One had wings, but no feathers. He wasn't the bird-reptile cross as Irix appeared in his demon form. This one looked like a plucked chicken with bumpy tan skin and a long sharp beak. Beady black eyes peered at me and he raised a featherless, narrow wing in my direction.

The other two were…weird, as if a plucked chicken wasn't weird enough. One was shaped like a hammer with stubby arms out either side of his long, tube-like body. The other resembled a bear with a lion head. They moved forward, crowding our personal space. I was trapped between the bear-lion and the wagon, trying to maintain my aloof elf vibe while acutely aware that these three could disembowel me with one swipe of a claw.

There was a flurry of conversation, then Rutter turned to me, his snout quivering. I got the impression that this wasn't going well.

"They're curious why an elf is wandering around outside of Patchine with a Low and a wagon, and they don't understand why you are dressed as a human."

"Are they going to hurt us?" I whispered, as if that would mask the fear in my voice.

"The high elves have all left, but they're not sure how powerful you are or if you have friends nearby. I don't think they'll kill us."

That wasn't exactly reassuring. Plucked Chicken poked me with a wing, nearly knocking me over.

Fear ran like ice down my back. "Tell them I'm a high elf, returned to…gather a few remaining things. That if they attempt to harm me, I will kill them. If they overpower me, my whole clan will hunt them down and feed them to the hounds."

Rutter scrunched up his eyebrows. "I don't think that's wise, Miss Amber. These are war demons. They're trying to weigh the fun they could have with us versus possible repercussions, but they would see a threat like that as…an invitation. War demons like violence more than they like sex."

Sex. At the thought of it my demon half rose to the surface, sizing up the three demons and liking what she saw. I'd been trying to conserve my energy since entering Hel, but I was getting ready to do a whole lot of genetic modifications. I'd need more than just what Kirby had given me, and I knew the humans in Libertytown weren't willing to have sex with a woman who looked just like one of the beings who'd enslaved them.

But demons? Especially demons that looked like…these creatures? I didn't care what my succubus wanted, that wasn't going to happen.

Rutter spoke for a moment with Plucked Chicken and Lion Bear, while Hammer circled me. I wasn't sure what to do. I could create lightning, but from what I'd been told all demons could. It wouldn't give me much advantage against these three, even with Rutter helping.

Sex. Do it. You need them.

Uh, no, I didn't. Sex with these guys would seem to be edging dangerously close to bestiality. Irix was a demon, but he'd always been in a human form when we'd made love. This was a plucked chicken, and a lion-bear. The only one with something remotely close to a human form was Hammer. While I was trying to determine if I could outrun them or super-grow tumbleweeds to encase them, my traitorous demon half sent out a wave of pheromones.

That got their attention, although I wasn't sure it was a good thing. Plucked Chicken's eyes grew big, his beak opening wide. I felt a featherless wing touch my shoulder, and Lion Bear reached out a furry paw to caress my arm. Crap. Maybe I should have just stood still and pretended to be an elf.

"They are amazed and very impressed," Rutter translated. "They think your elven form is extraordinary. They are conjecturing that you must have killed one and Owned its soul, since imitations are never this realistic. They are asking what household you are affiliated with."

"Um, the Iblis? I guess?" I thought of claiming to be part of Irix's, but I wasn't sure he had a household. Although as she was an imp, affiliation with the Iblis carried its own set of problems.

"I've told them that you have been in the human world for the last few centuries, which is why they don't recognize you. They are very intrigued and wonder if you would like to swap stories of conquest and valor over a bowl of roasted beaks."

And just like that I went from fearing for my life to being asked to…dinner? Or at the very least a sort of demon happy hour. This whole thing gave me an idea – a risky idea, but what the heck.

"I would be glad to join them another time, but I must get this wagon to Libertytown. I am trading some dwarven produce for a chicken wand from the Mage Kirby, and my elf button transported me too far from the city."

The war demons seemed quite excited as Rutter translated. "They love a good chicken wand, and can sympathize with the unreliability of elf-made magical devices. They hope that you will join them tomorrow night for beaks, and perhaps if you bring the chicken wand, they might also provide equal entertainment."

A party. I was a socialite in Hel. The demons turned to leave and I reached out with a tendril of pheromone, picking the one who looked most able to pull a wagon. I was probably going to regret this, but Lion Bear it was.

"Can you please ask the one with the lion head if he'll assist us in pulling the wagon to Libertytown? As a succubus, I am not physically strong, and he looks so powerful, as if he could tow a mountain with his shoulders. I would be very grateful for his assistance."

Gah. I was so going to regret this. Was my gratitude going to involve sex with something that looked like a Frankenstein animal?

The demon tilted his head, shaking his mane and pawing the ground. The other two slapped him on the back, appearing to congratulate him on his good fortune.

"He would be glad to help such a talented succubus. His name is Harkel, by the way."

The other two left to head off toward Patchine while Harkel grabbed the yoke and easily turned the wagon around. I'd picked well. The demon was pulling the heavy load through the sand as if it were an empty sled on snow.

It seemed rude to follow behind, so Rutter and I walked apace with the demon. I found myself reaching out a hand to run my fingers through his coarse mane and across the dense fur of his shoulders. Muscles bunched under my palm and Harkel made a low growl noise that seemed to signify pleasure rather than a warning.

Rutter shot me a perceptive look. "Miss Amber, I know you don't understand lots of things about Hel and demons, so I will tell you as we walk. Sex demons are very selective, so you don't have to reward Harkel with a sexual encounter. Often admiration, flattery, and caresses such as you are doing suffice."

That was a relief. "He won't hurt me if I don't have sex with him in return for his pulling the wagon?"

"Succubi and incubi usually only have sex with powerful demons and even then with restrictions. Most demons go through their lives never having experienced sex with a succubus or incubus. You can say no to him and he will respect that. Killing you would require him to pay a blood-price to our households. I don't command a high blood-price, but sex demons do."

Poor Rutter. And he said it so matter of fact, as if it was acceptable for my life to be more important than his.

The Low nodded encouragingly at me. "Sex demons aren't particularly strong, but they have specialized skills and nobody wants to push them too far. I doubt Harkel will attempt to rape you, since you'd tie him to you and if you're really pissed you could reduce him to an insane, masturbating monkey. For a war demon, that's worse than death. It's hard to create conflict when you're whacking off all the time."

I continued to stroke the demon's shoulder, my fingers twisting a piece of mane and tugging on it gently. I swear the demon purred.

"If I decided I did want to have sex with him, what would I do? How does this sort of thing work in Hel?" I asked Rutter.

The Low shot me a surprised look. "Well, if you're going for the classic, then he'll slobber on you, and stick his penis in-"

"I know that part," I interrupted. "I mean will he hurt me? What would demons consider to be a sexual encounter, and what sort of restrictions are typical for a succubus to require?"

Why was I even conjecturing about this? He was a lion-bear. But his fur was soft, and he clearly liked me. And to be honest, I liked him.

"You can tell him you'll consider sex only if he can manifest a human form, and no broken skin or bruises allowed. You can specify positions or how much physical contact. Anything." Rutter smiled encouragingly.

There was a moment in my life when I'd felt my succubus needs were a curse. I'd come to terms with that part of myself, but still worried over others' opinion of me. This was a demon. I was a half-demon. Maybe. But only if he had a human form, otherwise no deal.

The gates of LIbertytown came into view. Harkel pulled the wagon all the way to the granary where several of the town folk met us and began to unload the contents. Harkel shrugged off the yoke and stepped aside as he and Rutter exchanged a few words.

I needed to decide what to do. At the very least I owed this demon my gratitude. "I'll walk Harkel out," I told Rutter.

The Low tilted his head to blink at me. "Are you sure, Miss Amber? He seems an honorable sort, but I was told I should protect you."

"I'll be fine." I told him. Then extending a hand I waved for Harkel to come with me. Every few steps he would look over at me, his dark eyes reflecting the lights from the houses. He was huge – bigger than any bear or lion I'd seen in a zoo. His shoulder nearly came to mine, and his head was so large that on all fours he was the same height as I was on two legs.

"I really appreciate your helping me out," I told him, even though I knew he couldn't understand. There was something about him I liked. Yes, he was a war demon, but as Rutter had said, he seemed honorable.

"I wish you had a human form."

He just looked at me with those dark eyes and made that low growl noise deep in his throat. I did wish he had a human form, not to reward him for pulling the cart, but because I felt a connection with him. My succubus wanted him, and I did too. There was something about this war demon that I liked, but I couldn't get past the fact that he was a bear with a lion's head.

Once outside the gates I sat, and Harkel lay down beside me, his head in my lap. We sat there in silence, me stroking his fur with a rhythmic motion while looking at the moons and the stars in the dark sky. If this was all I could give him, all that we could share, so be it.

Suddenly my fingers were no longer petting fur, but stroking skin. I looked down in surprise to see a naked man, his head in my lap, my hand caressing down his neck. He turned to look up at me, the same dark eyes meeting mine. My fingers trailed along his shoulder, admiring the bulky muscles of his body, the warm, dark tan of his skin. His face was angular with long black hair tied into a knot and a narrow beard at the end of his chin. And those eyes – those dark almond-shaped eyes that knew stories and legends from long ago. I saw an army ride into battle, small groups raid and burn a city, Harkel holding a king's head in his upraised fist. I saw the blood and heard the screams, and felt the surge of adrenaline.

I should have been scared. I should have been horrified. But it all seemed right. When I looked into this warmonger's eyes and saw his proudest moments, I felt a kinship. Yes, he was a demon and he was capable of cruelty, of evil, but he also experienced loneliness and sorrow. He wasn't immune to hurt – either on the inside or the outside.

His fantasies spooled into me and I saw they weren't any different from the human fantasies I'd been fulfilling. Elves were cold, aloof. They acted superior, sneered at the demons who shared this world with them. I would be different. I would be the elf that desired him and admired him, that respected him, a willing and enthusiastic partner.

If I said yes. It was very clear to me that I was the one deciding how far this went. And so I decided.

Shifting my weight, I took Harkel's hand. He stood and tugged me up and into his arms. His lips were firm and demanding, his hands twisting my hair tight, but I knew in my heart that I was the one in control here. This demon could squash me like a bug, but he wouldn't. And his fantasies had less to do with rough sex and more about sensation.

His grip loosened on my hair and his fingers caressed along the edges of my ears. Then he let go, pulling his mouth away from mine and dropping his hands to his hips. This was his fantasy – a warmonger who strategized every move, planned each attack, and coordinated armies wanted to do nothing at all, to let me have my way with him while he just sat back and enjoyed.

My fingers traced along the muscles of his shoulder, across his chest and along the sides of his waist. Then they followed the rough V of dark hair to hold him in a firm grip. I stroked twice, then backed off, teasing him with my fingers, all the while watching his face. His dark eyes focused above my head off into the distance, his expression impassive. But the muscle that twitched in his jaw as well as the energy filtering into me told me he was far from unmoved.

He was about to be very moved.

I knelt down before him, tracing along his legs, then up the sensitive skin of his inner thighs. Then I took him in my mouth pushing him in deep before pulling back to kiss and nibble along his shaft and inner thighs as my hands worked him. I teased this way, bringing him to the edge, then backing off until I felt sure his knees would give out. All the while his hands stayed on his hips, his face unreadable except for his clenched jaw. Finally, I took pity on him and pulled him deep into the edge of my throat, matching the rhythm of my mouth with that of my hands until he came. The energy that had been winding into me suddenly became a torrent, nearly overwhelming me with its strength. It was beyond anything I'd ever experienced with a human. I felt it humming through me, and knew there was a lasting connection between us, a tie that would feed me energy for both of our lives. And it was completely voluntary on his part.

Only then did his hands leave his hips to caress my hair and ears. He murmured something and I rose, placing a quick kiss on his lower stomach on my way up.

"Thank you," I told him.

Like quicksilver, he changed back to the lion-bear form, and with a low growl and a nudge of his giant head against mine, he turned to leave. I watched him until the darkness of the night swallowed his form, then reluctantly went back into the city to Kirby's shop and climbed the stairs to my room. Rutter was already there, in his usual spot curled up on the chair.

"You're very pretty, Miss Amber. You glow now, all silver and gold." Rutter smiled at me. Yes, I was glowing, no doubt from the huge infusion of demon energy I'd just received.

"Thank you. I liked that demon quite a lot. I hope I see him again. Although I'm curious, how did you explain my inability to speak demon? Or Elvish?"

Rutter grinned. "Oh that was easy. I told them a sorcerer had summoned you a few centuries back, and although you were able to escape, you lost all of your language ability except for the one human dialect. They were amazed that you'd gotten away. Sorcerer summonings are the bane of every demon's existence."

A brain-damaged succubus. Well, if it kept me from being killed or enslaved, I'd play the part.

CHAPTER 8

After breakfast I locked myself in the bedroom at Kirby's house, first examining the eight varieties of root vegetables that Oleana Clawhammer had given me. They were very interesting, and I felt certain we were on the right path.

Next I went through the mountain varieties. Taking one of each sample, I modified the genetic structure to provide the best yield for the changing conditions in Libertytown. By lunchtime I was satisfied I'd found the perfect modifications. All I needed to do now was alter the rest of the samples, then help the humans here establish irrigation.

Which meant we needed to find the water. Kirby had assured me that they had augers and could extend them for deep drilling. The big question was where. And the answer to that question lay with the elves.

Setting the box aside, I dusted the dirt from my hands and went downstairs to find Kirby. Rutter had gone off to run a mysterious errand, and the mage was copying symbols onto small slips of parchment. I waited respectfully for him to finish. Finally, he looked up at me with a warm smile.

"Do you know which elven kingdom would have geologic surveys of this area? Specifically where the underground streams are as well as depth for any ground water?"

"To make well location and drilling more exact. Good idea." He thought for a second, tapping the end of the pen against his lips. "This particular portion of land used to be owned by Wythyn, so I'm assuming they would have been the ones to hold the records of any surveys."

"They wouldn't have taken the maps of Hel with them when they crossed the gates, would they? I'm assuming we can journey to one of the abandoned cities and find it in some kind of archive room?"

He tapped a finger on his chin in thought. "I'm sure they would have left those behind, but those cities are far from abandoned. There are still hundreds of elves in Hel who intend on remaining here indefinitely, as well as close to twenty thousand who haven't migrated yet, and they're mostly clustered in the capitals of the former kingdoms – which is where the archives would have been kept."

Great. Why couldn't they have been in an abandoned city? Or in a bunker just outside of Libertytown? "Are you on good terms with anyone there? Could we pay someone to give us the map?" I asked, hoping for an easy solution.

Kirby grimaced. "We do have some trade with the elves in Wythyn, but not at the level where they'd give us one. They're not just straightforward maps. Like everything the elves do, they're considered works of art and appropriately cherished."

"A copy then?" I was getting desperate. We couldn't just poke holes in the ground, drilling down ten thousand feet on a hunch. I could reach down into the ground to try to sense the water table, but not that deep. Plus, I wasn't sure if water would feel the same to me here as it did back home. We needed the map.

"Maybe. They're not always eager to trade those sorts of things with us. The request would be better received coming from another elf."

I saw where he was going with this. "I can't. I might look like one of them, but I don't speak more than five words of Elvish, and I've been told my accent is horrible. I can hardly claim laryngitis because I still wouldn't be able to understand them."

Also, I doubted that Rutter's sorcery-induced brain injury excuse would work with elves.

"Then I guess we try as best we can with what we've got. We can work on getting a map, and maybe manage to trade for it eventually."

Kirby set aside his work. "You look like an elf, but don't speak the language, so the best thing would be for you to sneak in and out without any of the elves seeing you. And I think I know just the demons to help you. Two greed demons. I don't do much business with them, but they've got a reputation as thieves. They, along with two other demons, pulled off a heist in Wythyn a few decades back that was legendary. The elves were furious. They never did recover the stuff these demons took."

Which meant they knew the kingdom, knew the capital city. And there was a good chance they'd know the layout of the building that held the maps. The only issue would be payment.

"What would they want in trade to escort me to Wythyn, help me steal these maps, and escort me back?"

"A few chicken wands and the chance to take whatever they can carry."

This might just work. "Think they'd be willing to leave first thing in the morning?"

Kirby grinned. "They're greed demons. They'll be more than willing."

CHAPTER 9

*R*utter found some elven-style clothing for me so I'd blend in if the worst happened and we encountered any elves. The 'dresses' were long strips of silk – spring green, sky blue, daffodil yellow, and a rich brown. One of the humans showed me how to wrap them around my body, then turned me to see my reflection in the mirror.

My bikini was more modest than this dress, but something within me snapped into place, like a missing piece of a puzzle. This was my elven half. This was who she was, and the revealing silky dress felt like a home I'd never known.

We met the two greed demons at the edge of the Wythyn forest. One looked as if he'd been in a horrible fire then rolled in red glitter. The other one was a giant snake with legs and arms. Not only did they actually know where the capital was, they knew where the archive building stood, and exactly what sort of protections the elves would have on the entrances.

We weren't two miles into the forest before the arguments began. The greed demons wanted to extend the project to include several other elven items not in the archives. Then they bickered over the best way to get through the city gates and past the building wards. Finally, I had to separate the two, Glitter walking slightly ahead with Rutter while Snake followed with me.

The greed demon grumbled something, then looked at me with his black eyes, darting a long forked tongue out of his mouth.

"He wants to know if he adds a favor or two to be redeemed at a future date if you would agree to have sex with him," Rutter translated. "He has always wanted to be with an elf woman and would be willing to trade either goods or services."

Absolutely not. For once the succubus in me agreed. Odd that I'd been fine having sex with Harkel, but this demon turned my stomach. It wasn't his snake-like form either. I liked snakes. This guy I didn't like. He was the expert, and I needed him to get in and out of Wythyn safely with the maps, but after that I hoped to never see him again. Something about him set off all my inner alarm bells.

"Perhaps another time," I told Snake, not wanting to outright refuse him. "I need to focus on getting the map and helping the humans."

"He says he has lots of energy to share. That he has magical items, gems, exotic foods. He'd be willing to assassinate one of your enemies in return."

"I'm tempted," I said trying not to shudder. "I just don't have the spare time right now. Perhaps in a few days when I'm done with the humans."

Snake didn't push the issue further, but his narrowed eyes made me wonder if he'd be more insistent on the way home.

"Miss Amber." Rutter tugged at my dress and one of my breasts nearly popped out of it. "You look just like an elf. Just like a glowy magic elf. If you knew the language, you could walk right in and get the map. Everyone would think you were one of the high ladies returned."

I doubted I could learn Elvish in the next six hours. Nyalla had been trying to teach me all year and I didn't even know enough to phrase a convincing greeting.

"Hopefully we'll be able to sneak in and out without any notice," I replied. "There can't be that many elves left behind. If there are a few hundred in the capital city, that's not many per square yard."

The further into the elven lands we got, the more I realized the extent of their modifications. How they'd turned the scorching desert with its acidic red soil into this lush forest was beyond my ability to comprehend. I could do small-scale plant modifications, but this... There were over eighty types of trees that I counted in one hour, along with hundreds of wildflowers, mosses, and bushes. Colorful lichens and fungus dotted downed trees, adding to the fairy-tale air of the place. Furry animals darted through the shrubs, and the birdsong was sweet and clear. It was like a Disney movie come to life. And all of it had been generated from a harsh unforgiving environment, held in place by the powerful magic of a handful of elves.

A cool breeze lifted my hair and I smelled honeysuckle and wild cucumber. This place was heaven. If I'd lived here, I'd never leave. Why had the elves decided to cross the gates when they had a paradise of their own creation right here?

Glitter put out a hand to stop us and we all held still as he listened.

"He says that we're far enough in away from the human settlements," Rutter translated when the demon finally spoke. "Any trespass wards we've tripped up until this point will be attributed to wandering humans or adventurous demons. The remaining elves won't spare the guards to come out this far and check on poachers, but as we get closer in to the capital, they'll know we're not just hunting durfts and they'll sound the alarm."

I bit my lip. "So what do we do?"

"We use these." Rutter grinned and dug in a pouch, pulling out four elf buttons. "One for each of us."

I'd discovered the joy of elf button teleportation just yesterday and was already a fan. "I'm assuming they'll take us just inside the wall around the city? We'll need to be stealthy, so we remain undetected until we reach the archive room."

"Yep. We'll need to be quiet and sneak through the streets to the archives. Once were there, the greed demons are going to get us in. We get the maps. They get whatever they want to get, then we leave."

"How are we going to get back?" I asked. "Aren't elf buttons one-use only?"

"These have two charges. One into the city. One back here."

I hoped there weren't so many elves in the city that we came across them, or that we accidently tripped wards, or that the goodies the greed demons wanted to steal had alarms or traps on them. And there was something else I was worried about. "I need to make sure I get the right map. Can you read Elvish?"

"No." Rutter's snout twitched and he turned to ask the greed demons.

Glitter looked insulted and spat out a reply.

"He says that he's a greed demon. He can read their script, and the elves will have all the archive documents neatly organized and labeled."

I was planning on getting all the maps pertaining to that section of Wythyn, just in case. It would be better to return carrying eight maps I didn't need then trust Glitter to point out the correct one.

CHAPTER 10

*I*nstead of taking us right inside the city wall, the elf buttons transported us to a lovely stable. It was nicer than my house. Chestnut beams and posts had been carved and gilded. The stall doors slid on whisper silent tracks, the bars shining with gold plating. There wasn't a hint of poop anywhere, and the whole place smelled of fresh timothy grass and alfalfa with the faint hint of leather and horse sweat. I pushed some loose hay aside with my foot and saw the floor was an intricate inlay of different colored woods making a mandala in each stall. The center aisle was also inlay, this one with a stylized tree of life. Every piece of wood joined perfectly, as if it had grown that way. The whole place shone.

While the greed demons checked to make sure the coast was clear, I plucked a piece of hay from my hair and straightened my gown. As beautiful and sexy as the strip of silk wrapped around my body was, the outfit wasn't all that practical for hiking through the forest or teleporting into a stable. It kept shifting as I walked, meaning I was always trying to shove my breasts back into the diagonal strip across my chest, and pulling on the lower section to ensure I wasn't flashing my crotch with every step.

"You like it here," Rutter commented. He'd been watching me ever since we'd entered the elven forest, and I got the feeling he meant more than the opulent stable.

"There's something in the air that makes me come alive."

"You're a half-elf. Maybe this is kind of your home? Hel. Wythyn. Both of them."

Probably. I felt as if I were a stranger but that this place was somehow my birthright. The demons scared me. I didn't know how to act around them, didn't know if they'd hurt me. Not being able to communicate with most of them added to my fear. And the elves would kill me if they discovered what I was. They murdered my mother, and that made me want to hate all of them, but somehow walking through the forest and even seeing this stable did feel like a homecoming. The whole thing felt like a homecoming, from the brief time I'd been here with Irix, to the moment I'd walked through the gateway in Columbia.

But as conflicted as I was, I couldn't deny that I yearned to fit into this world. I wasn't a half anything here. Normally I felt as if I were two beings, living in a weird sort of synergy within one body. Right now in Hel my two halves were in harmony.

We all made our way out of the stable, cautiously edging down the street from store to store. The capital was a ghost town, the perfect shops and homes starting the slide toward disrepair. A bit of paint was beginning to peel from a basket maker's sign. One of the cobblestones was loose on the street. Rain had stained a walkway where a downspout ended, and there was mud along the curbs. And the whole place was silent, as if the only thing that lived here were ghosts.

I knew there were still hundreds of elves in the city or

nearby, but we didn't come across any as we made our way to the archives. We edged around to a side entrance, and I watched while Snake examined the door. He spoke to Glitter for a moment, then took an amulet from a pouch and placed it against the door lock. Silver light streamed from the amulet until the entire door was bathed in it, then the light vanished instantly and I blinked to see once again a plain wooden door with metal banding across the top and bottom.

Snake stuffed the amulet back into the pouch and opened the door. Glitter took a gem from the bag at his waist, and threw it into the room. It bounced along the floor, clattering to a stop against something, but we heard, and saw, nothing else. The door wards must have been it, at least within this particular room.

We filed in and my eyes adjusted, seeing in the dark room as if it were daylight. Glitter went to the opposite wall and picked up the gem while I noted the thin layer of dust on the desks and the glass cabinets. There were writing implements and parchments neatly stacked on shelves, waiting for the elven archivists to return. It was weird seeing all this, like the elves had died in a sudden apocalypse and left this all untouched.

How had the elves found it so easy to make a new life in the human world, where the humans here couldn't? Although, come to think of it, I doubt the elves would find it all that easy. With their snobby pride they probably thought they'd have humans worshiping at their feet, feeding them grapes or some crap like that. In reality, they were likely to be living in a cardboard box under a bridge, and facing down a shotgun if they tried to demand subservience.

The sound of shattering glass had me reflexively dropping to the floor. The noise was deafening in the silence and I panicked, wondering if there was some sort of self-detonation ward on the building, or if the elves left behind had found us and were shooting into the building.

It wasn't either of those things. Snake had punched his fist through one of the display cases and was busy stuffing bejeweled pens and scrolls into a bag.

"Idiot," I hissed to Rutter, knowing that the demon wouldn't understand the slur. "They should have waited until we had the maps before they alerted every elf within two miles that we're here."

Now we needed to hurry. I stood up, frantically motioning to the others as I tried to remember what Kirby had said about the building layout. Through that door, down the hallway, then into the main room? I grabbed Rutter's hand and we followed the greed demons, expecting elves at any minute to burst through the doors and shoot us with arrows.

The hallway was long and sloping, but there was no mistaking the main area. We walked into the room and I stopped abruptly, staring open-mouthed. It was like a fantasy library. Four stories up with row upon row of books that lined the wall. Insanely tall ladders with wheels set in grooves were positioned against the walls, so the agile elves could reach anything they desired. The inner part of the room was a maze of three-foot-tall shelves and cases filled with books and scrolls. There were ornate cushioned chairs, long carved tables, artwork, and statuary. It smelled of oil paints, ink, and books. If I had thought the stables were amazing, this place was doubly so. The greed demons took off. I wandered the room with Rutter by my side, running my hand along the top of the shelves and cases which were still dust free. Did someone come in here to clean and maintain the place? This held all the history of Wythyn, their lineage, their maps, their stories.

I belonged here. There was a noise of breaking glass and I

winced. The greed demons most definitely did not belong here, and I regretted Kirby's promise to allow them to loot the archives. This place was sacred, holy. I had to let them steal some statues and gems, but I couldn't let them carelessly toss the history of my mother's people aside to be trampled underfoot.

"Miss Amber," Rutter tugged on the edge of my dress. "Be careful not to trip any wards. There might be poisoned darts or some other security measure on the cabinets. I don't want you to be dead."

Shit. I froze. Snake had already made a ton of noise breaking the glass, and we'd been like elephants stampeding down the hallway. Any ward we tripped probably wouldn't matter at this point, but getting jabbed by a poisoned dart wasn't on my to-do list. Plus, I had one problem.

"I can't read any of this and the greed demons ditched us to grab statuary," I whispered. "All the scrolls look the same. I don't know which ones we need."

Rutter twisted his hands together, looking from me to where the sound of laughter echoed through the room. "I'll go get them."

The Low ran off. I heard him arguing with the other demons then a squeal of pain that made me clench my fists. If they'd hurt Rutter, I'd...shoot them full of lightning, or trap them in a giant bush of thorns, or sex them to death. None of which sounded very threatening, but I didn't exactly have much in my arsenal that would help me take down two demons that were older and far more powerful than me.

I heard footsteps, then saw Glitter arrive with Rutter. The little Low had a cut on his cheek. I glared at the greed demon, but he ignored me, shifting his half-empty sack to the other hand as he read the signs.

"He says that these are all histories. There's a section in the back that says it's for maps."

Rutter and I followed Glitter. He continued to mutter words under his breath that the Low did not translate for me. I was pretty sure they were complaints. Or curses.

"Can you ask them to be careful when stealing things?" I asked Rutter, hating to put him in the middle of something that might get him more than a scratch on his cheek. "I don't want them to damage the books and scrolls."

I looked up to see Rutter's panicked expression. "I…I can't, Miss Amber. They're greed demons and I'm just a Low. And you might be a half-succubus, but you're young. They'll do whatever they want and we can't stop them."

I bit my lip. "They can take the statues, gems, and paintings," I told him. "I just don't want them to trash the place, to disrespect the stories of my mother's people."

The Low's eyebrows shot up. "I thought the elves were not your friends, Miss Amber. I thought they wanted to kill you, that they'd killed your mother."

They had. They'd murdered the woman who dared to conceive and bring a half-breed child to birth. They wouldn't hesitate to kill me if they realized what I was. But still, this place held a part of me, of my heritage.

"They're just old books," Rutter added. "They mean nothing."

Maybe not to him, but to me they were like roots that tied me to the firmament. I might never read these. They might eventually decay and turn to dust. But I couldn't let them be torn and trampled. I couldn't.

But I couldn't let Rutter take the heat for my decision. Communication might be an issue, but as soon as I got the maps, we were leaving. I'm sure whatever the greed demons had collected by then would be sufficient. It would have to be.

We followed Glitter through the maze of shelves to the back wall of the room where a series of glass cabinets held gilt-edged books. The greed demon, his eyes glowing, read the labels on the cases, then waving me back, he slammed his fist into the glass.

Nothing happened except Glitter's fist bouncing back and nearly hitting me. The demon looked around then picked up a statute, wielding it like a baseball bat. It was a really beautiful statue of a dancing woman. I hissed "no" and put my palm on the case to keep him from smashing the statue against it.

The glass vanished leaving books and scrolls open on their shelves.

"Wow. Look at that, Miss Amber. Guess you're elf enough for the wards."

Glitter grunted something, then stuck the statue in his bag and ran off, leaving me to assume that the maps I wanted were in this case.

I reached in, holding my breath in case my hand blew off or the scrolls turned into scorpions and bit me, but nothing happened. They were just scrolls, maps. Yes, they might be beautiful works of art, but compared to other items in the archives they probably weren't of great value.

My fingers closed around them, feeling the heavy dry parchment, the silk ribbons that bound them closed, the crisp feel of them in my hands. With great care I placed them in my bag – every last one of them since we didn't have time for me to sort through them and figure out the correct one, even if I could read Elvish. Then on impulse I took the book that was in the case on a shelf above the scrolls. It would have smashed the scrolls in my bag, so I kept it in my arms clutched against my chest.

Alarms sounded, lights flashed. I looked down at the book, then at the empty case in confusion, wondering why we'd set off the wards now and not when I'd grabbed the scrolls or opened the case. Maybe the demons had tripped the alarm with their careless looting.

I looked around to see Glitter and Snake heading toward the entrance. Glitter was stuffing items into sacks along the way, while Snake was knocking over shelves, kicking the books into the air as he laughed.

"Not the books," I shrieked, trying to be heard over the alarms. Snake turned to look at me, then with his eyes fixed on mine he pushed a shelf over with his shoulder. I watched in horror as dozens of books fell, spines dented, pages crumpled and torn. The shelf landed on top of them, crushing the books underneath. Picking up one, he ripped it in half, tossing the pages about like confetti.

I handed the bag with the scrolls and the book to Rutter and stomped toward the greed demon. I should have been worried about the maps, about ensuring we got safely out of here and on our way back to Libertytown, but all I could see was the damaged books scattered on the floor, Snake's sneering face as he picked up another one and ripped it in half.

I lost it. Grabbing a nearby statue, I ran over and waved it at Snake. "Steal all you want, but don't trash the place. And don't tear up the books, you stupid fucking oaf. Don't damage the books. Get out. Get out now."

Snake snarled, rising to his full height. Then he grabbed the statue and twisted it out of my hands. "Get out. Now," he mocked me in badly accented English. Then he hit me across the head with the statue. I staggered to the side, feeling blood running down the side of my face and into my eyes.

"Miss Amber!" Rutter shouted.

My hands went up to guard against a second blow and I felt myself blasted with a shot of energy that threw me backward into a bookshelf, blackening my shoulder. Books fell, one particularly heavy one hitting me on the head.

Everything suddenly seemed to move in slow motion. I heard Rutter's scream as Snake picked him up and threw him into a display. Through a red haze of blood, I saw the glass splinter as Rutter crashed through the case. I saw Glitter racing for the door. I saw Snake coming toward me with the statue raised to strike. I saw the torn pages on the ground, filled with beautiful calligraphy in a language I couldn't read.

I got pissed. More than pissed. I reached out my hand toward the greed demon, curling my fingers into a fist and then letting them fly open.

The demon's serpentine face froze mid laugh. His feet elongated, toes multiplying and tearing through the inlay of the floor. His legs fused together, scales melding into a hard pattern of grooves and notches. His torso stretched, arms extending outward as they twisted and turned. The last to change was his face, open mouth gnarled into a knot on the trunk of a misshapen, barren tree.

Rutter scrambled to his feet, staring at Snake in shocked amazement. I pulled my hand back and looked at my palm. I'd just turned a demon into a tree. It wasn't a particularly pretty tree, but then again Snake hadn't been a particularly pretty demon.

I'd gotten angry and turned a demon into a tree. At that moment I vowed that if I ever saw Pele again, I'd never give her shit for doing the exact same thing to the men who'd spurned her centuries ago.

Wow. I was no different than Pele. I was no different than a vengeful, capricious goddess.

"Miss Amber! Oh, Miss Amber, are you okay?" Rutter knelt down next to me, his hand touching the side of my head, then the horrific burn on my shoulder. Was I okay? Shouldn't he be asking if Snake was okay? Had I killed the demon? Was there a way to turn him back or would he spend the rest of his life as a tree? Where was Pele when I needed answers to these questions?

I was an elf. Normally I could heal myself, but when I tried all that happened was I stopped bleeding, and the terrible burn on my shoulder became a mess of blistered, angry red flesh. I was exhausted, drained. Evidently turning a demon into a tree had completely tapped me out.

"I'm fine," I lied. I still hurt, my head throbbing, my shoulder feeling as if it were on fire. That was the least of my worries right now. "Are you okay? He threw you into that glass case."

Rutter nodded. I examined him carefully and saw only superficial cuts. Relief flooded me. I wasn't sure Lows could easily heal themselves, and I certainly couldn't help him beyond basic first aid at this point.

"Miss Amber, you were amazing. I had no idea you could do something like that." Rutter turned to admire the tree.

I had no idea I could do something like that either, and I wasn't sure what the repercussions would be. "I shouldn't have done…that. Will I go to demon jail? Am I going to owe a blood-price to his household?"

"I won't tell if you don't, and somehow I don't think the other demon is going to say anything either." Rutter walked over and spat on the tree. "Good riddance. He was going to kill you, Miss Amber. If you hadn't turned him into a tree, he would have killed you. Do you know what he said about you? That you were weak, that beyond a decent elf-form you were worthless and only good for fucking. He was wrong. You're scary-strong. Nobody should mess with you."

Evidently not, or they get turned into a tree. The Low's words did make me feel better about what I'd done to Snake, and his admiration was very flattering. Still…a tree. Would he ever turn back into a demon? Would he be a tree forever?

In spite of my shock over what I'd done, we still needed

to get out of here, so I leaned on the fallen bookshelf and got to my feet, grabbing the book and bag of scrolls from where Rutter had tossed them. I turned around to speak to the Low and saw him fall, an arrow sticking out of his leg. A bundle of rope hit him and shot out into a net, surrounding Rutter and pinning him to the floor. Looking around I saw half a dozen elves, bows at the ready, arrows notched and pointed at me.

I put up my hands unsure what to do. It was pretty incriminating that I was holding a book and a bag of scrolls. Actually it was pretty incriminating that we were in the archives at all. The elves stared at me in shocked silence, then began to whisper amongst themselves. They still had projectiles pointed at me, so I kept my hands up. The whole time I tried to come up with a good way to get out of this situation. I couldn't run for it and leave Rutter behind, but I was pretty sure if I knelt down to get him out of the net, I'd get shot. Could I heal from whatever was in those elven arrows? Probably not, even if I were at full strength. With no other option, I just stood motionless, holding a book and a bag up in the air. Maybe I could turn them all into trees?

One of the elves put down his bow then walked closer to me and asked me a question. I had no idea what he'd said and my interpreter was inside a net and shot with an arrow. The elf repeated his question and I lowered my hands to point down at Rutter.

The elf shook his head, then motioned toward the tree smack in the middle of the archives. I motioned toward the tree, made little devil horns on top of my head, then pointed at myself.

The elf's eyes about left his head. Again I waved a hand toward Rutter, pointed at my open mouth, then made talky motions with my fingers. He stepped back a few paces and motioned for me to remove the net. The other archers took aim, and I was well aware that one wrong move from Rutter and they'd turn him into a pincushion.

Slowly I peeled the net back. "Don't move," I told him.

"I can't, Miss Amber." He grimaced. "They shot me in the leg. It will be paralyzed for a few hours. I'm sorry, I'm not going to be able to run. If you get a break, go."

"I don't need you to run for it, and I'm not leaving you. I need you to be an interpreter."

He raised his eyebrows, his snout wiggling.

I patted him on the shoulder. "They haven't shot me yet. I think they don't know what's going on. I look like an elf, but I can't communicate with them. They're reluctant to shoot me, or even arrest me. If you translate exactly what I tell you, I think I can talk us out of this."

Rutter scooted clear of the net, dragging his one leg behind him. The arrow stuck out of his furry thigh and I resisted an urge to pull it out.

"I'm ready to translate, Miss Amber," he told me.

"I am Amber Shania Lowry and I have returned to Hel so that I can retrieve some of our archives to preserve our heritage in the new world."

The Low translated, and the non-bow wielding elf stepped forward once more.

"He wants to know why you can't speak or understand Elvish. You are clearly a High Elf, royalty if you were the one who transformed a demon into a tree. What has happened to you that you have lost your language?"

Time to lie like...well, like a demon. "I must be honest with you, the new world is not as we expected. The humans there are powerful, and our magic is not reliable on the other side of the gates. They have metal boxes of death that race at us faster than the quickest horse and flatten us like a boulder. They have metal and wood sticks that shoot spelled projectiles, and we are unable to heal from the injuries they cause.

We thought we would rule, yet we find we are barely able to survive." I clutched my throat dramatically. "One of the sorcerers stole my knowledge of Elvish, leaving me to communicate only with this inferior human language. Thank the Goddess I escaped with my life."

Bows hit the floor as the elves clapped their hands against mouths and cheeks, wailing in sympathy. I soaked it in, as if I were a martyr.

"I cannot return to live here at this time. Not when so many of my people suffer under the cruel hands of the humans. I came back to retrieve our stories in hopes that the past might give us guidance on how to prevail. When I arrived with my demon interpreter, I found several greed demons stealing treasures and destroying the archives. One escaped, but one I caught and punished." I pointed dramatically to the tree.

They stared, open mouthed. Then they looked at the tree.

One spoke, and Rutter turned to me. "He wants to know why don't the high lords return? The elves need you here. They need the High Elves. They need their family. They beg the elves to return to Hel and leave the humans to their horrid land."

I smiled sadly. "I cannot abandon my people. The humans have imprisoned many of them, and the angels have turned against us. One day, we will return, but not until we *all* can return."

"They want to know what they can do to help." The elves were aghast at my speech, wringing their hands. I felt as if I were a lead in a Greek tragedy.

"Maintain the archives. Wait for us. We will return."

I had no idea if the elves would return, but it sounded better than 'see ya, have a great day.'

The leader of the group nodded.

"He sees that you have the ceremonial rites and records

tome. Do you also want the history of the elven migration to Hel? That along with prayer might give you insight."

Shit. Would this guy believe me if I told him that the human sorcerer had also taken away my ability to read Elvish? Luckily I didn't have to bluff that one because the guard led me to a glass case with a huge, ancient book inside. He stood aside, obviously waiting for me to do something.

As before I put my palm on the glass and nearly passed out with relief when it vanished. I reached for the book, but found my hand stopped by an invisible force field.

The elf said something in hushed tones.

"Only royalty can take the book," Rutter told me. "It's a blood lock."

My heart fell. They thought I was a High Elf, that I was royalty. If I couldn't get the book, would they imprison me? Would they kill Rutter?

"Wasn't your mother cousin to the High Lord, Miss Amber?" Rutter asked. "Try to use your blood, and hope it actually works."

I bent down to pick up a piece of glass and holding my breath, I jabbed my index finger. A red drop welled. If this didn't work, we'd run for it. I'd grab the bag of scrolls, half drag Rutter, then try to lightning bolt as many elves as I could. And we'd run.

Here we go. I extended my hand toward the book and tried to keep from trembling as I reached the point where the force field had stopped me before. The drop of blood sizzled. A cube surrounding the book glowed gold. My hand passed through. Careful not to get my blood on the book, I took it and brought it into my arms. The thing was heavy – far more heavy than the one clutched in my other arm. I didn't like the idea of carrying both of these all the way to Libertytown, but this was my cover.

As soon as the book was in my arms, the elves knelt, bows

and arrows on the ground. Rutter crawled over toward me, touching the hem of my dress. "Can we leave now? Before they figure out what the other half of you is?"

Maybe. We still weren't out of here. "Are they going to expect me to teleport away? Will they believe I'm some sort of royalty if we stroll out of here and into the woods – me carrying two heavy books and you dragging a numb leg?"

Rutter grabbed the edge of a bookshelf and pulled himself upright, his left leg dangling from his hip. "I'm going to tell them that you need a moment to pray, to experience once more the beloved land you foolishly left behind, to promise the Goddess that you have renewed your commitment to create a paradise for your people whether here or in the new world."

"You're good," I told him. Damn, for a Low the demon sure could think on his feet.

Rutter relayed the speech. The elves nodded, two of them coming forward to support the demon's weight on their shoulders. Taking a deep breath and lifting my head, I picked up the bag of scrolls in one hand, shifting the weight of the two books in the other, then walked in my most regal air from the room, down the hallway and this time out the front door.

CHAPTER 11

In the morning every muscle ached. Rutter and Kirby were surrounded by scrolls when I came down, hot beverages and the remains of breakfast nearby.

"Please tell me you didn't get porridge all over the scrolls," I scolded, placing my bag on the floor.

Rutter grinned up at me. "Did you sleep well, Miss Amber? Is your shoulder and head healed?"

No. For that I'd need to have sex, but right now I had more pressing matters than my injuries or my lack of energy to attend to. "I'm fine. I want to hear about the scrolls. What do they say?" I went to peer over Kirby's shoulder even though I couldn't read a thing. They were beautiful, with creamy parchment, inky black script, and colored symbols and drawings all along the edges. They reminded me of the medieval illustrated manuscripts I'd seen in the museums.

"I found the one with the locations and depths of the ground water and springs. We'll drill this afternoon and should have irrigation water by tonight. I'm thinking we should consider a secondary well for drinking water in case the one we have now goes dry."

That was amazing news. "How about the others?"

"Ley lines and results from a geological survey, but check this one out." He shoved a parchment under my nose.

"Groundhogs in space with parsley?" I guessed, eyeing the drawings.

He snorted. "They're incantations for keeping animals away from certain plants. I think they used it not just in gardens, but in sections of the forest, such as holy spaces, where they didn't want rodents eating up all the sorrel."

"That might come in handy. Do you have the proper ingredients? Is that a spell you could cast?"

He shook his head. "It's not a spell, it's a ceremony that the elves perform. It requires the magic they carry within them. Ours is compatible, but not quite the same. That's why the elves kidnapped us and made us slaves. We could do magic they couldn't, but they can do quite a lot that is completely out of our reach."

"Well, I'm an elf and I clearly can do elf-magic sorts of things. I wonder if I could perform the ritual?" I leaned closer Kirby's shoulder to look at the scroll, which still appeared an artistic pattern of undecipherable script."

"You don't know Elvish. I could translate for you, but I'm not sure if these have to be in their language or not. And I don't know if you speaking the words would help if you didn't truly understand them. I'm thinking there has to be something beyond just this ceremony, something that gets passed down from high elf to high elf." He rolled up the scroll and set it aside. "I've never seen any of these performed. They were sacred ceremonies, not meant for human eyes. I'm not even sure the other elves were able to witness them either. High elves are very secretive about their magic."

It was a shame I didn't know any elves. If I was a full elf with my mother's heritage, I'd know this stuff. I'd be able to help the humans far beyond modifying a few plants.

Although if I were a full elf, I might not care about the humans.

"I also grabbed two books from the archives and I've got no idea what they are beyond that one has ceremonies and the other has stories from the migration to Hel."

Kirby jerked his head to look at me in surprise. "Stories of the migration? Those are only available to royalty. How did you… oh."

"I guess half a royal elf is good enough."

"I'm not sure I'm comfortable having them here," Kirby confessed. "It feels sacrilegious."

I waved toward my bag. "I'm going to ask Nyalla to translate for me. And it's probably time for me to knuckle down and make a serious attempt to learn my mother's language."

Kirby glanced at my bag then up at me. "So you're leaving?"

"I'll be back in six months," I assured him. "There's nothing else for me to do right now, and I've got an internship this summer."

The mage stood and walked us out, shaking my hand once we reached the door. "Thank you for coming to help us, Amber. I'm not sure if this will be a permanent solution, but at least we don't need to worry about starving for the next year or two."

Hopefully I could think of something more long-term in the meantime. I said my goodbyes and Rutter and I walked out the city gate and through the hot desert. The gate shimmered before us, like a mirage.

"Come see me if you're ever on the human side of the gates," I told Rutter. "Will you be here to help me again when I return in six months?"

He smiled and nodded. "If I'm still alive, I'll gladly assist you again, Miss Amber."

My heart wrenched. Life as a Low was an uncertain one. And his words reminded me of something else he'd said.

"Rutter, you've been a wonderful guide and translator. You're smart, brave, loyal, and your quick thinking saved me with those demons near Patchine as well as with the elves in the archives. Lows *are* worthy of a succubus' attention. I'd like to show you that."

I reached out to sense his fantasies once more and got… nothing. It wasn't like the murky confusion of Kirby's amulet. This was as if the Low had no fantasies, yet I knew he did. I'd sensed them outside the dwarven city.

"You already have shown me that, Miss Amber. You've already fulfilled fantasies that mean far more to me than just sexual enjoyment. A higher-level demon cared enough to worry about my safety, to come to me when I was hurt, with concern and the desire to help me. You treated me with kindness and affection. *Those* were my deepest fantasies."

I reached out to run a finger down the top of his snout. "So, no boinky-boink?" I teased.

He grinned. "Maybe next time, Miss Amber."

"Next time," I assured him. Then I adjusted the bag on my shoulder, feeling the weight of the books inside, and stepped through the gateway to my home.

ACKNOWLEDGMENTS

A huge thanks to my copyeditor Jennifer Cosham whose eagle eyes catch all my typos and keep my comma problem in line, and to Damonza, for cover design.

Most of all, thanks to my children, who have suffered many nights of microwaved chicken nuggets and take-out pizza so that Mommy can follow her dream.

ABOUT THE AUTHOR

Debra lives in a little house in the woods of Maryland with her sons and two slobbery bloodhounds. On a good day, she jogs and horseback rides, hopefully managing to keep the horse between herself and the ground. Her only known super power is 'Identify Roadkill'.